DISASTER

André Du Pres felt the shudder as a jagged limb ripped into the canoe, and a second impact as it rose behind him. The canoe was being pulled under, impaled and trapped. He threw himself into the water, fighting to stay free of the rolling tangle.

"Over here! This way!" yelled the frantic Pale Star.

André did not see the blow coming until too late. He had called out to Star, and saw her turn to look, when a whirling limb of the great tree rose from the water directly in front of him. The jagged tip struck him hard across the forehead.

Consciousness was fading fast as he slipped beneath the surface. The water was warm and welcome. There was a sense of letting go, there was no more need to fight. Then there was only darkness. . . .

RIV

D

Bantam books by Don Coldsmith.
Ask your bookseller for the books you have missed.

River
of
Swans

》》 》》 》》 》》 》》 》》 》》 》》 》》 》》

D O N   C O L D S M I T H

BANTAM BOOKS
TORONTO · NEW YORK · LONDON · SYDNEY · AUCKLAND

All of the characters in this book
are fictitious, and any resemblance
to actual persons, living or dead,
is purely coincidental.

RL 6, IL age 12 and up

*This edition contains the complete text
of the original hardcover edition.*
NOT ONE WORD HAS BEEN OMITTED.

RIVER OF SWANS
*A Bantam Book / published by arrangement with
Doubleday*

PRINTING HISTORY
*Doubleday edition published September 1986
Bantam edition / February 1989*

ISBN 0-553-27708-1

Published simultaneously in the United States and Canada

*Bantam Books are published by Bantam Books, a division of
Bantam Doubleday Dell Publishing Group, Inc. Its trademark,
consisting of the words "Bantam Books" and the portrayal
of a rooster, is Registered in U.S. Patent and Trademark
Office and in other countries. Marca Registrada. Bantam
Books, 666 Fifth Avenue, New York, New York 10103.*

PRINTED IN THE UNITED STATES OF AMERICA

O   0 9 8 7 6 5 4 3 2 1

Time period: Middle seventeenth century, shortly after
PALE STAR. Number 10 of the Spanish Bit Saga.

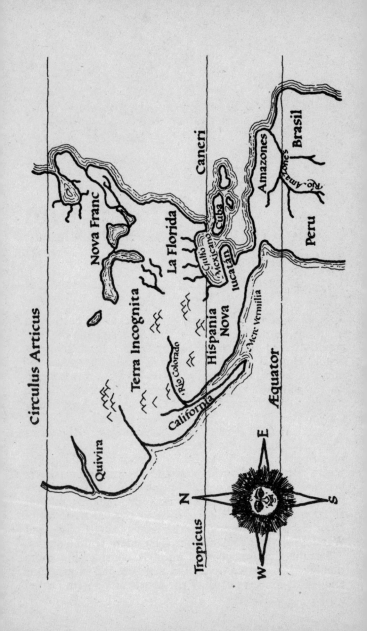

Introduction
By Loren D. Estleman
》 》 》

As a western writer (who hopes one day to be spoken of in the same breath with Don Coldsmith), I'm frequently called upon to defend my lifelong Michigan residency. How, it is asked, can someone who makes his home in a rural area forty miles west of Detroit hope to understand the philosophy and conditions of life on the frontier? As often as I've answered the question, I continue to be appalled at the ignorance it betrays.

The American West as it is commonly perceived lies to the left of the 98th meridian, a cartographer's line bisecting the North American continent at the point where the eastern forests end and the prairie grasslands begin. This arbitrary device relegates to the East nearly half of Kansas and Texas and most of Oklahoma, as well as a portion of the Dakotas roughly equivalent to all of Utah. By this reasoning, all the James Gang's post-Civil War depredations took place in the eastern United States.

Fortunately, the popular mind is considerably more flexible than the compass and sextant, and is generous enough to conceive of all of the above, along with Daniel

Boone's Kentucky and the tales of James Fenimore Cooper, despite their upstate New York settings, as western. (It should be noted that when Horace Greeley offered the counsel "Go west, young man," he was referring to New Jersey.) Michigan is not so fortunate. This is especially difficult to comprehend in view of its history, so accurately presented in *River of Swans*.

The Northwest Territory, of which Michigan's two peninsulas represent the greatest land mass, had witnessed many a weary transient by the time Antoine de la Mothe, Seuer de Cadillac, set foot in 1701 on the western bank of the river known by Indians as the Crooked Way and declared, "Here I shall build a city!" Some 20,000 years before Detroit glimmered in his opportunistic eye, the first of many bands of what we are now privileged to call "native Americans" made their peripatetic way here, either eastward across the fabled land bridge from Siberia or northward from South America—depending upon which anthropologist one credits. Sac, Fox, Huron, Mohawk, Potawatomi, Mohican, Assiniboin, Iroquois, Ojibway, and a lost race known to history only as the Copper People paddled their canoes along Bloody Run and the Au Sable and hiked around Saginaw Bay in search of game and enemies.

Thousands of years behind them, from the East, came the explorers, carrying their parfleches from tall ships to pack trains to bateaux and canoes pieced together from sinew and birch. Among these was the legendary Étienne Brulé (doubtless a source of inspiration for the Brûle of this story), sent ahead by Champlain to scout out the St. Lawrence Seaway and trade with the nomadic tribes who populated New France; and this he did faithfully for twenty-two years, an eager and adventure-loving figure known from Duluth on Superior's western shore to the northern Copper Country to New York State, living many lives until the day his luck ran out in a Huron camp and he was bludgeoned to death.

He was neither the first, nor decidedly the last such casualty in the Michigan wilderness. By the time those pioneers whose experiences are most closely associated with the westward migration began their journeys by

Conestoga to the Oregon homestead country and the goldfields of California, their way had been paved by the United States Cavalry; a century and a half earlier, when those who would settle Detroit set out for Michilimackinac, they would meet in the American Indian a warrior who had never known defeat.

They came originally looking not for gold or freedom, but for the fabled new route to Asia, that glittering lie that drove Columbus to Puerto Rico and ultimately into madness, and that, like Ponce de Leon's Fountain of Youth and Hernando Cortez's Seven Cities of Cibola, lures Coldsmith's André Du Pres from the *ennui* of garrison life down into the Conradian Heart of Darkness in pursuit of an armchair commander's crackpot dream of a Southwest Passage. Thus, from Balaklava to Montgomery's campaign in the Netherlands, have the delusions of men in power wrought needless tragedy and necessary gallantry.

River of Swans follows a time-honored tradition in taking its engaging protagonists downriver in search of—what? Home, freedom, riches, adventure, or merely the Country Beyond the Hill. Odysseus, Gulliver, Marlow—and inevitably, Huck and Jim—understood that it was all of these things if it was one. Jonathan Swift's Brobdignagian giants and Mark Twain's Duke and the King had nothing on Don Coldsmith's scalphunters, and the great winds which when released from their sack swept the seafarers of Homer's *Odyssey* to the ocean's farthest reaches just when they had drawn within sight of home were scarcely more devastating than the storm that shatters the Du Pres expedition. But it is the constant movement from the familiar ever deeper into the unknown that tugs at Coldsmith's readers as it did those adults and children of Industrial Revolution America who gathered on streetcorners to read *The Adventures of Huckleberry Finn* in the Chicago *Times* and *Century* Magazine. As Glendon Swarthout, another storyteller of our time, put it, in *Bless the Beasts and Children:*

. . . For this is the marrowbone of every American adventure story: some men with guns, going somewhere, to do something dangerous. Whether it be to scout a continent in a covered wagon, to weld the Union in a screaming Wilderness, to save the world for democracy, to vault seas and rip up jungles by the roots and sow our seed and flag and spirit, this has ever been the essence of our melodrama: some men with guns, going somewhere, to do something dangerous.

Coldsmith states it more succinctly:

   This was the world to which André had aspired. Adventure, discovery, the romance of strange sights, sounds, smells, and experiences. . . .

In a work of such basic atavistic yearnings as *River of Swans*, one can read any number of literary allusions. Du Pres's readings—Rabelais, Calvin, and Descartes—are as seminal to the wisdom he will gain in his journey as were Milton and Goethe to the synthetic man in Mary Shelley's *Frankenstein*; and after all, was not that cobbled-up wretch searching for nothing more than home, as is Coldsmith's Pale Star? One cannot resist parallels between the dubious relationship of darkly seasoned Brûle to impressionable, naive Du Pres to those of Dickens's convict and Pip in *Great Expectations* and Long John Silver and Jim Hawkins in Stevenson's *Treasure Island*. Closer to home, compare it to young Bob Starrett and the eponymous hero of Jack Schaefer's *Shane* and the mutually nameless pilgrim-narrator and mentor-cowhand of Owen Wister's *The Virginian*, the twin classics between which American western mythology remains staked to this day. The theme is as simple (although never simplistic) as the frontier itself: When East meets West, anything can happen.

   There is, of course, the requisite loss of innocence—a staple from Tolstoy to Hemingway—and a rebirth for Du Pres, appropriately symbolized by the pervading presence of rushing water. To be reborn, one must first return to the womb:

Consciousness was fading fast as he slipped beneath the surface. There was a sense of letting go, a release from the necessity to fight any longer. The water was warm and welcome, and he wanted to relax.

Then there was only darkness.

His world when at last he opens his eyes has changed forever, as has he, and as, in *War and Peace,* had Prince Andrei while staring up at the vaulted sky above the head of the ultimately insignificant Napoleon. How fitting, given this comparison, that Coldsmith should choose to nickname his hero Sky-Eyes.

But dissection of art is a fraud, pretending in its obsession with nuts and bolts to understand the soul. For the essence of a Coldsmith novel is its soul, as supported by its narrative compassion and its lyrical minimalism. Can one read the epistolary openings of *River of Swans'* late chapters, containing Du Pres's conscientious use of "The Moon of Roses" and "The Moon of Storms," without divining the full depth of his wide-eyed character? The death of Cloud should be required reading for every would-be writer who insists upon shedding the reader's tears for him; and I would direct the attention of the authors of the past five Pulitzer novels to the subtlety displayed in the simple line: "The songs of mourning were sung for three days, and then the People resumed the ways of the living."

I have digressed from my thesis: Michigan, and all those western lands no longer associated with the frontier, here restored to their heritage by the tenth book in the elegiac Spanish Bit Saga. The subject has been beatified by Hemingway, Philip Caputo, and Jim Harrison; documented by John Steinbeck and Bruce Catton; and shafted by William Least Heat Moon, who should know better, being himself a native American. In New York City and Los Angeles, home of garbage strikes, serial killers, and breakdancing, a videotape of a handful of Detroit troublemakers setting automobiles ablaze to celebrate a World Series victory is piped over national airwaves as evidence of a city gone mad. The western writer, who alone remembers that civilization was old in Michigan when Philadelphians were still picking fleas off one another's backs, remains our last hope for a seminal place in the history of our country.

The novitiate, who holds in his hands for the first time a Don Coldsmith novel, is to be envied the worlds that are about to open for him. The veteran who has followed the Spanish Bit this far and who may fret that he has seen too much of a good thing, need worry no longer; it is this writer's belief that *River of Swans* is Coldsmith's finest work to date. It is my distinct if somewhat redundant pleasure to assure everyone who has had the patience to reach this point in the introduction that he has made an excellent choice.

—Whitmore Lake, Michigan
June 1988

Author's Note
» » »

In the seventeenth century, the French were pushing westward along the Great Lakes, establishing forts and trading posts as far as present-day Michigan. An expedition under La Salle in 1682 traveled down the Mississippi to its mouth. There they claimed the entire watershed of the great river, naming this substantial portion of the continent Louisiana, after their monarch, King Louis XIV.

Though history tells us little, it must be assumed that prior to this time, limited French probing expeditions would have tentatively challenged the mysterious New World. History would not record the failures, or the fate, of the expeditions that simply vanished, swallowed up by the vastness of the unknown.

This is a story of one such ill-fated expedition.

1

》》》》》》

André Du Pres sat with his back against the rough logs of the hut and watched the activity in the compound. His stool was tilted back on two legs so that he could stretch his long shanks out in front of him.

It was spring, and Lieutenant Du Pres was both bored and restless. He had looked forward with anticipation to his assignment on the frontier. He had been disappointed in most respects. There was very little of the wild adventure he had expected.

Instead, here was a land in which it seemed everyone had gone mad. Fort Mishi-ghan was the farthest west, the most remote, of the chain of French outposts. It was critical, he had been told, that they push westward ahead of the English.

Each nation had its own tribes of friendly natives, who made war on the other group and on each other. They were paid in trade goods for each enemy they killed. Proof of such a kill was the scalp, the hair from the top of the deceased one's head.

This was an efficient means of tally, André conceded.

However, the custom had deteriorated. With the price of scalps high, there were many cases of fraud. There were jokes based on the fact that it was possible to produce up to five or six valuable scalps from a single well-haired head.

In addition, there was no proof as to *whose* hair was involved. Rumor had it that there were those who killed indiscriminately, selling the scalps to the highest bidder.

So far, André had seen no combat, but he had been at this outpost only a few weeks.

He missed the niceties of civilization, his books, the social interrelations of polite society, the women in their tightwaisted full skirts, elegant at some seasonal social event. Yes, he had to concede, perhaps he missed the dances most of all.

There was one girl in particular. He had danced with her on the night before he left for New France. Babette, whom he had known since they were children, had suddenly grown to maturity. She had bumped against him, accidentally, it seemed, as they left the dance floor. She'd murmured an apology, but her eyes said coquettishly that the collision had been quite intentional, and promised much more.

He could still feel the excitement of the warm curves of her body against his for one fleeting moment. How he would have loved to repeat that sensation, to prolong it. Her inviting expression, demure yet flirtatious, had strongly suggested that it was possible.

How, André now wondered, was she spending her time this season? He could imagine her in the soft, perfumed spring of his distant homeland.

Was she flirting with some other young officer in his absence? Probably. They were actually only slightly acquainted. He had no right to expect the girl to share his fantasies.

But it was frustrating anyway. He shifted position and scratched his back against the logs. The sun was warm through his linen shirt.

He wondered what sort of spring his parents were experiencing, back in Flanders. With a little nostalgia and just a trace of homesickness, he thought of his mother.

She would be setting out her garden about now, he estimated, a variety of flowers and kitchen vegetables. Her herb garden had long been the envy of the entire area.

Perhaps it was from his mother, André reflected, that he had inherited an inquiring mind. Though many people still thought a woman should not be educated, Marie Du Pres was an avid reader. André's father, retired now from a military career, encouraged her interests.

The two did not always agree. Since his childhood, André had listened to their discussions. There were a number of books in their home, far more than in most families of comparable means.

There were a few very old books, treasured by Marie. André had read extensively during his formative years, and one of his favorites was a well-worn copy of Rabelais's *Gargantua*. A story about giants, it was amusing yet serious. The young man had found it comforting, because the writer seemed to have faith in a basic good in everyone. This approach was much like that of his mother.

It was not true, of course. Not entirely, anyway. In fact, André wondered sometimes if another writer, preacher John Calvin, might not be more nearly right. The writings of Calvin, equally well-worn, spoke of the basic corruptness of human nature.

Young André had been somewhat confused by these contradictory theories. It had, however, forced him to think. In part, his mind was still not entirely settled on the subject. He was certain that Rabelais's ideas of basic goodness were unrealistic, but they appeared to be so much more fun than those of Calvin.

André's parents had never pushed him directly to accept any particular view. Sometimes he wished they had, rather than forcing him to think on his own. Making one's own decisions, however, was a favorite topic of his mother's. In her last letter, in fact, she had written in glowing terms of a new philosopher whose work she had been reading. His name was Descartes, and his views on the power of human reason, Marie assured her son, were certain to be important.

André had chuckled when he read the letter. How

could his mother comprehend the scarcity of philosophy and human reason here in the wilderness of New France?

But perhaps she could, he reflected. Her family were Huguenots and had been badly persecuted. Her grandfather, in fact, had been killed in the riots. Marie could remember only bits and pieces of the strife that had plagued her childhood. She was outspoken in praise of the monarch who had brought peace and tolerance to France. Henry the Huguenot, in line for the throne, had first brought peace by joining the Roman Church. Then, following his coronation, the new king had declared freedom of religion for all.

There was still active disagreement between Catholics and Huguenots, but no violence.

Henry IV was dead now, but King Louis XIII had continued the policies of tolerance. Europe was stimulated by the challenge of the New World, and France was moving rapidly into a major role in its exploration. Ships returned to France and England laden with furs and tobacco.

This was the world to which André had aspired. Adventure, discovery, the romance of strange sights, sounds, smells, and experiences. And here it was, dull and boring, and he was restless and depressed and homesick.

André rose, stretched, and wandered aimlessly around the stockade for a little while. Then he sauntered outside the main gate. He noticed a group of about twenty natives seated on the ground, listening to a priest through an interpreter. Out of curiosity, André moved in that direction to lean against a tree and observe.

The Jesuits, he knew, were extremely active at the forefront of exploration, converting the natives to their brand of Christianity. It might be amusing to watch. The priest was doing a good job of telling the familiar story of Creation, the fall from Grace, and Salvation. He spoke in French, and a native interpreter then translated for the seated listeners. There were occasional exclamations of approval.

André noticed that the interpreter also used the hand-sign language. That had been a thing of great interest to him. It was apparently a universal language among the natives, composed of signs made with the hands and

fingers. Any natives, even those who understood nothing
at all of each other's tongues, could communicate. How
useful, André had observed. He must learn this skill if he
was to remain assigned on the frontier.

The priest finished his instruction, and there was a
general murmur of approval. Then a young woman rose
to her feet, apparently to ask questions. André had not
noticed her before in the blur of seated people. Now she
could not escape notice.

She was tall and straight as a pine. Her bearing was
that of royalty, the look in her eyes like the gleam in the
eyes of eagles. She reminded him somewhat of a sleek,
hot-blooded horse.

André could see her face from the side, a sculptured
beauty of profile. Large, wide-set eyes and prominent
cheekbones gave way to firm yet sensitive lips.

The young man gasped at her beauty. Surely, he thought,
this must be the most attractive woman he had ever
seen. He must know more about her.

2

》》》

André glanced around and saw one of the other officers standing nearby. He strolled over, trying to appear disinterested.

"Who is the woman?" he asked casually.

The other man glanced at him and chuckled.

"You have not seen her before? That is Pale Star, wife of one of the scouts. She is beautiful, no?"

André nodded, eyes riveted on the girl. She had shifted the bright-red trade blanket that she wore, and settled it artfully over her shoulder, freeing both hands. Now she prepared to use sign-talk.

"She killed a man once, with a throwing-ax," the other officer was saying in André's ear. "It was just before I came here."

André was wishing the man would be still, so that he could pay complete attention to the young woman. She was preparing to speak, waiting for the audience to quiet.

"Now watch," said the other officer. "This girl is one of the best storytellers at this post."

His comment was needless, as André's entire attention

was absorbed by the girl's stark beauty. Now she began
to speak, slowly and distinctly, accompanying her words
with hand signs so that all could understand. Her voice
was deep and vibrant, with an exciting throaty quality, a
compelling tone that made a listener give undivided
attention.

The most amazing thing to André Du Pres, however,
was that she spoke in his own tongue.

"She speaks French?" he asked his companion in
amazement.

"Yes, and several other languages, too," chuckled the
other man. "She has a natural gift for it, apparently. But
then, she has been here three or four years."

The two soldiers quieted to listen to the girl. Her
French was not perfect. Her wording was a trifle clumsy,
and she had a persistent, though by no means unpleas-
ant, accent. These flaws were more than offset by the
strength and conviction of her delivery.

"It is good, my chief," she addressed the priest. "I have
liked your stories, especially the part about the real-
snake and the apple. Rising from the dead is good, too."

The priest smiled patronizingly.

"Thank you, my child," he almost purred. "And what
is your name?"

"He is new here," chuckled André's companion, "or he
would know."

"I am Pale Star, my chief."

"It is no matter, child, we will baptize you and give
you a Christian name."

The girl seemed to ignore this last, and proceeded in
her talk, using signs also.

"My people live far away, down the Big River and
beyond. At the time of Creation, they were in the center
of the earth. They came out, First Man and First Woman,
through a hollow cottonwood log."

The priest stood numb, his mouth falling open in a
look of startled despair. The other officer nudged Du Pres
in the ribs with an elbow and chuckled quietly.

Pale Star continued her story, oblivious to the various
reactions.

"One of our almost-gods, the Old Man of the Shadows,

sat on the log and tapped it with a stick, like a drum, and the People crawled out into the world, blinking their eyes at the light."

There was a quiet stir of interest among the seated listeners. Now the face of the priest was distorted with rage.

"Stop!" he shouted. "This is blasphemy!"

He turned to the seated listeners.

"You must not listen to this. It is superstition, it is bad!"

The frustrated interpreter was trying to translate the rapid staccato of the priest's tirade. The onlookers stared in wonder, not understanding.

Pale Star, too, seemed puzzled.

"My chief," she began firmly as the priest paused for a moment, "I have listened to your Creation story, and I have said it is good. I do not understand. You do not wish to hear mine?"

"No!" the priest almost shouted. "You speak lies! I offer you salvation, and you ridicule the Blessed Saviour with lies and blasphemy and superstition."

It seemed probable that the native girl did not know the meaning of the words, but she maintained her dignity. She realized that she was being chastised and her dark eyes flashed fire. Despite her anger, she maintained her composure. When she spoke, her voice was calm, but a trifle tense.

"My chief, you are very rude. We listened politely to your stories. Now when it is my turn, you do not wish me to speak."

With a dramatic gesture, she swept her blanket around her.

"I will listen no more to your stories, either!"

She turned and strode away, followed by a murmur of approval from the seated natives, who had followed her sign talk.

"Do not listen to her," shouted the frustrated priest. "She is guilty of blasphemy!"

Now even the interpreter seemed confused and in doubt. He did not even try to translate. The assembled natives began to rise and shuffle away.

"Wait! I will tell you more!" the priest called after them.

The departing listeners did not even look back. André's companion was leaning against a pine, roaring with laughter, while tears rolled down his cheeks.

"I do not understand," André questioned. "You have seen her do this before?"

"Yes, once," the other panted weakly, "but not this well."

He broke into another spasm of laughter, holding his sides as if in pain.

"But what—" the frustrated André sputtered.

"Look, my friend"—the officer struggled to regain composure—"you have to understand their customs."

"Yes?"

"Well, when different tribes get together to trade or make talk, they tell stories."

"But—"

The other waved him down impatiently.

"It is their custom—a trade. You tell me your stories, I tell you mine. It keeps things interesting. But he did not know—"

He collapsed into another spasm of laughter.

André began to understand. He could see the humor in the situation, and he chuckled politely. Other emotions were more powerful in his mood, however.

First, he had found himself very sympathetic to the point the girl was trying to make. Raised in a home with different religious faiths, André had been well schooled in open-minded tolerance. He rather liked the little he had heard of the native custom of freely exchanging stories. He had never encountered anything quite like this before, a free exchange of ideas without prejudice. He must see more of this.

By far the most intense emotion, though, was admiration for the girl Pale Star. Here was a young woman, at a disadvantage in the confrontation, who had accounted well for herself. Pitted against a sophisticated, well-educated aristocrat, not even really accustomed to the language, she had still risen to the challenge. She had not only risen, she had met the authority figure on his own ground, and had beaten him. Yes, any onlooker would have had to agree. The adversaries had clashed, the skirmish was over very quickly, and the winner was clearly this incredibly beautiful native girl.

André had never been so attracted to a woman before. He wondered if her husband had any idea what a treasure he possessed. Then he immediately felt guilty for the thoughts he was having about another man's wife.

3

» » »

Du Pres spent most of the next day thinking of the girl Pale Star. His thoughts covered a wide range of emotion. He was not certain what excited his attention the most, her intellect, her spirit, her beauty, or, sadly enough, her unavailability. Confusion and frustration were the final results.

To make matters worse, he seemed to encounter the young woman everywhere he turned. How strange, he thought. He had been at Fort Mishi-ghan three, nearly four weeks, and did not recall seeing the girl until yesterday. Now, he saw her constantly.

He strolled down to the lakeshore and met her as she carried water. She was there, unexpectedly, as he walked across the compound toward the trading post. That time she had smiled at him. Just an open, friendly smile, not anything sensuous or provocative, but a smile. It had stimulated his interest beyond belief, and in turn his own reaction irritated him. What was the matter, he wondered, that he could not control his own thoughts?

It was a great relief, therefore, when he was summoned

to the presence of the commandant. A blue-clad soldier
knocked respectfully at the door of the hut that André
shared with two other junior officers.

"Lieutenant Du Pres?" the man inquired.

"Yes. What is it?"

"Monsieur, Captain Le Blanc requests your presence."

"Of course."

He swung his long legs from the bunk and shrugged
into his tunic. It was a formal summons, and he should
be in uniform. He buckled his sword belt around his
waist and picked up his hat.

"I am ready."

The soldier turned without speaking, and started across
the compound toward the commandant's house. Du Pres
followed. He was ushered into the captain's presence by
the orderly who made a terse announcement.

"Lieutenant Du Pres, monsieur."

He turned and left the room.

André glanced around the office quickly. He had been
here only once before, on the day he arrived. It was
hardly an office, even. A rough desk, a couple of chairs,
and another chair behind the desk, in which the captain
now sat. Spread before him on the desk was a litter of
maps, books, and papers. The officer seemed preoccupied, and Du Pres saluted and remained at attention.

The captain returned the salute halfheartedly, remaining seated. He seemed totally absorbed in the papers on
his desk. Finally he seemed to notice the figure before
him.

"Oh yes, at ease, Lieutenant. Please be seated."

He pointed to a chair.

"Thank you, sir."

The captain stirred the papers and came up with one
that he studied at length.

"Ah yes, Du Pres. I have been looking at your record.
You have done well at the academy."

André was becoming annoyed. What was this all about?

"Yes, sir. Well enough."

"Somewhat better than that," observed Captain Le
Blanc. "You are not one of those young officers whose
commission is bought with his father's influence."

"I hope not, sir."

"No, definitely not," the captain mused. "You may be my man."

"I do not understand."

"Ah, I was thinking aloud. Let us talk, Du Pres."

"Very good, sir."

"Du Pres, do you know what we are doing here?"

"You mean why I am in your office, sir?"

"No, no. Why we are here at Fort Mishi-ghan."

André shrugged, perplexed.

"Why the troops of King Louis are here on the frontier," the captain continued.

"Well, the fur trade, I suppose?"

"Yes, yes." The captain nodded excitedly. "But there is more. Tell me, Du Pres, you have heard of the Northwest Passage?"

Of course, André told himself. How stupid, not to see where the captain was leading him. It was one of the great theories of the century.

"Oh. Yes, sir." He nodded.

"The Great Northwest Passage," the captain continued dreamily, "the pathway to India."

Du Pres recalled that when explorers first landed in the New World a century and a half earlier, they had thought themselves in India. What was the man's name? Colombo, or some such. Italian, but sailing for Spain. Ever since, a passageway through or around the continent had been sought. There must be a way, a shortcut to the wealth of the Orient.

Early explorers had sailed up the river they now called the St. Lawrence. When the chain of Great Lakes was found, it was felt that this must be the secret, the passage through the land mass. There were those who wondered at the fact that the Lakes were fresh water, not salt. It was true, however, that exploration had already penetrated perhaps halfway through the continent, and still the natives told of lakes beyond.

The captain spread a map on the desk and beckoned to André.

"Look, Du Pres, we are here."

He stabbed a forefinger at the map, which appeared to

be a general outline of the northern continent of the
New World. André could not fail to notice that most of
the detailed notations and geographic features were along
the coasts, where ships had probed the strange land. The
interior was mainly blank and white, with mountains
placed here and there at random. The mapmaker had
frankly labeled the vast bulk of the continent "Unexplored Wilderness."

André followed the captain's pointing finger. At the
southern tip of a large body of water appeared a small
cross, an X-mark that may have been added later, after
the map was made.

"There," said Le Blanc, "is Fort Mishi-ghan."

Du Pres saw that the lake was one of some half dozen
sketched across the continent and connected to the western ocean. The placement seemed arbitrary, and no other
geographic features were in evidence. He had seen maps
such as this before, in which the wishful thinking of the
mapmaker was reflected.

"This is the Northwest Passage?" he asked cautiously.

"No, this is all wrong. All the maps are. I want to
show you something else. Du Pres, may I have your
pledge to secrecy?"

"Of course, sir."

The captain leaned back in his chair, and the dreamy
look appeared in his eyes again.

"My boy, I am entrusting you with a dream. You know
that it is important that we, not the English, find the
water passage to India."

André nodded, still embarrassed that he had not immediately seen the point that the captain was making.

"And those who make the discovery will be rewarded
with riches beyond measure."

"I suppose so, sir."

"Du Pres, I have been on the frontier for fifteen years,
six of them here. I have begun to have a feel for this
land."

He paused a moment.

"Close the door, Du Pres, and then come here."

André complied, a trifle uneasy at the bright glitter of
enthusiasm in the eyes of the other.

"Look, now, at the map," the captain continued. "I am about to show you something I have shown to no one."

Now the young man was becoming even more uncomfortable. This did not appear to be a part of a routine military assignment. He was not certain he wanted to share the captain's secret.

"Why me, sir?"

"Because I like your record, Lieutenant. You thought it was an accident that you were assigned here? No. I served under your father, and I have watched your progress. I requested your assignment, because I wanted you for a special mission."

André's neck-hairs began to prickle just a trifle. It was flattering, of course, but there was a tiny voice of warning. What if his superior was a deranged dreamer with grandiose ideas, dangerous to those under him?

The captain was beckoning now.

"Come, I will show you. I want to send you to lead a party of exploration."

The little voice of warning whispered again, but the call of the unknown was louder.

"Yes, sir?"

"To put it in perfectly simple terms, Lieutenant, I have discovered why no one has found the Great Northwest Passage. They are looking in the wrong place. Now, look here at the map."

He indicated again the area of Fort Mishi-ghan. Now André became aware that there were several marks that had been inked in on the map, not originally there. They appeared to be rivers or streams, several of them, running roughly parallel to each other.

"See," continued the captain, "in the past six years, I have charted the headwaters of these rivers. Do you see their direction?"

"Yes, sir. Southwest."

"Right. Du Pres, every river in this area flows southwest. Do you see what this means?"

"Not exactly, sir."

"All right, then look here."

He pointed to the left side of the map. There the

outline of the continent was detailed, the coastline meticulously rendered by the artist.

"See this?"

The captain pointed to a narrow gulf in the southwest. A long finger of land ran parallel to the coast, forming what was almost an inland sea. André leaned forward to read the small letters.

"Vermilion Sea," he murmured.

Under that title was another, in smaller lettering: Sea of Cortés. At the northern end of this gulf, a river was depicted, the Colorado, running into the gulf from the interior. Then, again, the frustrating white wasteland, "unexplored."

"Now look at the map, at the unexplored area." The captain was pointing eagerly.

His finger, practically trembling with excitement, traced the general direction of the streams of Mishi-ghan. Across the white unexplored areas, southwest, on and on across the map.

"Somewhere, here, they flow together, they converge, Du Pres, and become this river, flowing into the Vermilion Sea."

"But—"

"Lieutenant, look at it. The Great Northwest Passage, which has never been found. And why? Because they have always looked in the wrong place."

He drew close, and lowered his voice confidentially.

"It is not a Northwest Passage," he whispered confidentially, "but a *Southwest* Passage to India."

4

>> >> >>

"**B**ut, sir," André protested, "that is clear across the continent, and the southern coast is claimed by Spain."

"Ah, yes, for the present," agreed Le Blanc, "but if we can prove . . ." He paused a moment. "Would you prefer that I ask someone else?"

"No, no, sir, I did not mean that."

"Good!" laughed the captain. "I thought I had chosen my man well."

"Thank you, sir. When do I start?"

"Tomorrow, if you wish."

André nodded. It would be good, he reflected, to be away from the influence of the girl Pale Star. He had forgotten her for a time in the excitement of the discussion and the mission. Perhaps he could put her out of his mind entirely while on such an exploratory journey. The challenge would stimulate his thoughts and busy his waking moments.

"Very well, sir. How many men?"

"Only one, and a scout. You may choose your man. The scout is to be Brûle. You know him?"

17

"No, sir."

"He is the best. Most trustworthy."

"He knows of the mission?"

"Not all. No one but you and I know that. The others are to know only that it is a long scout to the south and west."

"How long, Captain?"

"As long as it takes. You need not go as far as the ocean. Just far enough to prove the theory. Who knows? Two years? Three?"

Le Blanc shrugged indifferently.

"Do you have someone in mind that you wish to take?"

André had been thinking along those lines.

"Anyone I wish? Officer or noncommissioned?"

"Well, yes," the captain replied.

"Very well, sir. Sergeant Cartier."

Cartier was quiet, thoughtful, and a thoroughly competent woodsman. Though only a noncommissioned officer, he was self-educated, could read well, and possessed good judgment. André had noticed him before they even arrived at Mishi-ghan. Cartier had been on the frontier for a number of years.

"Good choice!" nodded Le Blanc. He opened the door and called to his orderly.

"Jacques! Bring Brûle and Sergeant Cartier."

He returned to the desk and began to roll up maps and papers.

"You wish to leave tomorrow?"

"Yes, sir, if you think we can be ready."

Le Blanc shrugged.

"We will ask Brûle. You can draw whatever supplies you need at the store."

The orderly returned with two men. André nodded to Cartier and turned to meet the scout.

"Lieutenant, this is your scout, Brûle. I think you know Sergeant Cartier."

Everyone nodded and exchanged glances, Cartier ill at ease. He was the only one present, André realized, who had no idea of the purpose of the meeting.

Brûle was well built, with dark curly hair, dark complexion. Only his light gray-brown eyes betrayed his mixed blood. He had a quiet, friendly smile and André liked him immediately.

It was growing dark now, and Le Blanc's orderly brought a candle.

"Close the door," the captain called.

The soldier did so.

"Now," began Le Blanc, "Cartier, you are to go with Lieutenant Du Pres on a scouting mission."

The sergeant nodded.

"How many men, sir?"

"Only you two and Brûle."

Cartier's eyes widened just a trifle, but his expression remained unchanged.

"Yes, sir."

"This will be a long mission, several months. Brûle, can you be ready to start tomorrow?"

The scout looked slowly and carefully at the others.

"Yes, sir, but dawn the next day is better."

"Of course. You can plan tonight, assemble your equipment tomorrow. Satisfactory, Lieutenant?"

André nodded. This was happening awfully fast.

"With the Lieutenant's permission," Brûle said, "it would be better if you both wore buckskins."

"Good. Can you find them some?" Captain Le Blanc asked.

"Yes, sir. I think so."

He sized up Cartier and Du Pres, in their impractical blue uniforms of wool and linen.

"I will bring them tomorrow."

"Good. I have told Lieutenant Du Pres: Draw what you need from the store. Anything else?"

The three shook their heads.

"Very well. Dismissed! Du Pres, you stay a moment."

The others passed into the gathering twilight and Le Blanc closed the door again.

"Any questions?"

"No, sir, I think not. I may have some later, before we leave."

"All right. Now, Brûle knows it is to be an extended

scout. Cartier knows nothing except what we have said
in this room."

"Is he to know more?"

"At your discretion, but I would wait until you are
well on your way."

"Yes, sir, my preference, too. Brûle?"

"Again, your discretion. He already knows all but the
actual goal."

"Then I see no reason."

"Good. That was a good suggestion of his about the
buckskins. Ever worn them?"

"No."

"Comfortable. Best, though, you won't be marked as
French. Not right away, anyway."

André nodded.

"Anything else, Lieutenant?"

"I think not, sir. May we talk again before I leave?"

"Of course. Oh, one more thing, Du Pres. Brûle's wife
will go with you. Her tribe is from somewhere in your
direction."

"Brûle's wife?"

"Yes. Perhaps you've met her. Pale Star, I think she is
called."

5

>> >> >>

Du Pres rummaged through his belongings and brought out a slim, leather-bound booklet. It had been a gift from his mother at the time of parting.

"You must keep a journal of your stay in the New World," Marie had told her son.

He had stuffed the notebook hurriedly into a pocket and had scarcely looked at it since. What few events seemed worth recording had occurred when the note-book was not at hand. It had remained in the bottom of his valise. Someday, André promised himself, he would bring the journal up-to-date, but the occasion had never come.

Now he unwrapped the waterproof oilskin packet, took out the book, and opened it. The smooth, creamy texture of the blank pages seemed to call for some sort of action.

André laid aside the letter he had just finished and addressed to his parents. He carefully repointed his pen and uncorked the vial of ink again. Very slowly and deliberately he began to write.

* * *

Anno Domini 1640, and of the month of April, the fourth day: I, André Du Pres, Lieutenant in His Majesty's service, do begin this journal.

He paused in thought for a few moments, and then continued.

This will serve as a log, or account of a special mission to which I am assigned. At dawn tomorrow, I depart for the unexplored territory to the west.

He paused again.

I will be accompanied by Sergeant Cartier, and our guide will be the scout Brûle, who is also known among the natives as Hunting Hawk.

This time the pause was even longer. Finally he heaved a deep sigh and returned to the page.

With us will also be the wife of Brûle, a native woman who is called Pale Star.
I will reveal more of the nature of this mission in due course of the journal.

Now satisfied, he waited a few minutes for the ink to dry, and rewrapped the oilskin packet tightly. He included a couple of short goose-quills and a tightly stoppered small vial of ink. It pleased him to think that he was now well prepared to document their exploration.

He fumbled in the unfamiliar loose folds of his new buckskin tunic and placed the oilskin bundle in one of several pockets he found there. Brûle had cautioned that they must travel light. Each would carry a backpack, but only necessities.

One item André did elect to take. His father had presented him with a pistol of the latest type. Italian in manufacture, it featured a spring that could be wound with a clock-key. When a lever was released, a steel disc rotated rapidly against a flint, throwing sparks into the pan to ignite the powder. This eliminated the necessity of carrying a burning match, frequently dangerous to the gunner as well as to his target. André had fired the gun only a few times, but much to the amazement of his fellow officers.

Dawn was hardly breaking when the little party set off. Captain Le Blanc had risen to see them off, sleepy yet excited. He shook André's hand firmly.

"Good luck, Lieutenant. I expect a good report."

"Yes, sir."

"I do not know when to expect you back. Take all the time you need."

"Very well, sir."

"You have trade goods to buy canoes or whatever you need."

André shifted the heavy pack and nodded. He was beginning already to question the wisdom of carrying his pistol, powder, flints, and lead balls.

"We go now," stated Brûle simply. He turned and strode into the morning fog, followed by the sergeant. André quickly moved after them, and the girl brought up the rear.

It was full sunlight before the scout called the first rest stop. The travelers gratefully removed packs and sat down to rest. André rubbed an already sore shoulder.

"If the Lieutenant would not mind a suggestion," Cartier offered respectfully, "your pack will balance better a little higher."

He assisted in the adjustment of the pack straps, and André settled back again. He was trying to avoid staring at the girl. At close range, she seemed even more beautiful than he had thought at a distance. Emotion ran so strongly in him when he looked at her that he was afraid the others would notice. Yes, it would be best to avoid her company all he could.

It was a strange mixture of feelings that had swept over him when he learned of Pale Star's participation in their mission. There was a thrill of excitement at the thought that they were to be together, in daily contact, for several months. Close on the heels of that thought, however, came the other. How difficult to see this woman every day and realize that she would always be inaccessible to him. An odd wish crossed his mind, a desire that this couple, Brûle and his wife, would not demonstrate much affection. André felt that that would be more than he could stand.

The next moment he chided himself for such a ridiculous thought. Perhaps it would help if he became close to the scout.

"Brûle," he began, "could you teach me the sign-talk?"

"Why?"

"It may be useful. I think we should all know sign-talk."

Brûle nodded in satisfaction.

"It is good. We will teach you each evening. It is not difficult."

Cartier nodded.

"I would learn, too."

"Of course. But I think my wife should be the one to teach you both. She is very skilled in sign-talk. It is used more farther to the west, among her people."

He turned and glanced inquiringly at the seated girl. She nodded.

"It is good," Brûle said again. "We start tonight."

6

>> >> >>

"**H**ow are you called?"

The two soldiers clumsily made the signs, copying Pale Star's lead.

"Yes. That is good. Three signs. The first, 'how.' "

She made the hook-finger sign for a question.

"Now, this sign is not only 'how,' but 'where' or 'when,' *any* question."

The two nodded.

"Next, 'you.' Simple. Just point. Then the sign for 'speak.' See? A finger pointing out of the mouth."

They practiced for a moment.

"Now see if you can tell what I say."

She made the signs. To his amazement, André understood instantly. The first sign was obvious, the second they had just learned.

"I—am called—"

It was obvious that the remaining gestures constituted her own name.

"I am called Pale Star!" exclaimed Cartier in delight.

"Yes," nodded the girl. "Now, another word or two. Here is 'water.' "

She extended a hand, palm down, and made a horizontal fluttering motion, like flowing water. Then she preceded the water sign with the question sign.

"Where is the water?" André and the sergeant chorused together.

"Good!" Star clapped her hands in delight.

She seemed so like a child at times, André thought. At others, like royalty.

"Now, here is the sign for 'woman.' "

She made a sweeping motion down the side of her head, as if brushing her long hair. Of course, thought André. Perfectly obvious.

"Man" was designated by two fingers pionted down, indicating a person's legs. Several signs were fairly obvious. Food, hunger, sleep, spear, bow, knife. House, home, or lodge was indicated by crossed forefingers, simulating rafters or poles. André began to amuse himself by inventing phrases.

"Where is your home?"

"With Hawk," she answered, using both words and signs, "buy my tribe lives far away."

He saw a twinge of sadness in the dark eyes.

"How are you here?" he signed.

"I was stolen as a child. Someday I will go back."

She did not even us the signs.

Hunting Hawk glided silently into the clearing and dropped an armful of wood near the fire.

"It is quiet," he observed, "but we will stand watches. I go first."

He sat down for a moment to chew a strip of dried meat and warm himself by the fire. The early-spring evening was quite chilly.

"How is the sign-talk?"

"It is good. They learn quickly."

Hawk nodded, pleased. He rose, took his robe for warmth, and slipped into the woods again.

"Hawk is your man," signed André, practicing his new skills.

The girl nodded.

"Where is your woman?" she signed.

The question-sign was so flexible that he was not certain. The girl could have been asking "Who is your woman?" or even "Have you a woman?"

This seemed for a moment to be a major flaw in the sign-talk. But no, he realized, the answer to all these questions would be the same. He smiled in understanding and signed in return.

"I have no woman."

She smiled.

"You learn sign-talk quickly, Sky-Eyes," she signed.

"What did you call me?" he asked aloud.

She laughed, a beautiful sound like running water over pebbles.

"You did not know? Of course, who would tell you? Sky-Eyes. It is the name the people around the fort gave you when you came."

"Why?"

"Everyone has a name."

"But why Sky-Eyes?"

"Your eyes are the color of the sky."

"And Sergeant Cartier?"

"He is the Woodchuck."

André glanced at the sergeant, who was grinning broadly.

"You knew this?"

"Yes, Lieutenant."

With his heavy jowls and prominent front teeth, André thought, Cartier does look a little like a woodchuck. *Mon dieu*, these people have a way of coming straight at the heart of a matter, he told himself.

"We should sleep now" the girl was saying.

She took her blanket and rolled in it beyond the fire. The two men followed suit.

André lay a long time, wide awake and thinking. He saw increasing trouble with his feelings for the girl. At first he had noticed her remarkable beauty, then her pride and spunk. Now he began to see that she had other admirable qualities as well. She was, he saw, a highly intelligent woman, with a clever sense of humor.

In the brief lesson in sign-talk, he had begun to value her friendship highly. Yet he knew that what he was capable of feeling for this remarkable woman was more than friendship. What he *already* felt for her, he had to admit. Yes, there was no way he could stop at friendship.

He realized the danger involved all too clearly. This woman, it had been said, had killed a man with an ax, under circumstances with which André was unfamiliar. Such a woman might be very dangerous to a lover if she was displeased. Yet, it seemed so out of character for this gentle little girl-woman.

Then there was the danger represented by her husband. Even if the girl might be unfaithful, which seemed unlikely, a man would be a fool to risk the wrath of Brûle. His reputation as a deadly fighter was well known.

In addition to all this, André was beginning to like and admire the man and his skills. It had been a long while since he had felt such confidence in a pair of companions such as Hunting Hawk and Cartier. Woodchuck. He smiled to himself.

Any strain on the respect that the three men had for each other would place a strain on the success of the mission. Possibly, it could be disastrous.

No, the others must never know of his feelings for the girl. Especially she must never know. He would unscrupulously avoid her except when absolutely necessary. He would take pains never to be alone with her, so that there could be no doubt in anyone's mind. His mission would depend on it.

Why did things have to be so complicated? There was none of this uncertainty and frustration in his relationship with Babette, now so far away.

Of course, he realized, the childish flirtation of the immature Babette could hardly compare with the regal quality of a casual conversation with this princess among women.

He dozed fitfully until someone shook him by the shoulder.

"Wake up, Lieutenant. It is your watch," whispered Brûle.

André rolled out quickly and stood up, yawning and stretching.

"It is quiet," Brûle continued. "Too close to the fort, I think."

The mere presence of a fort, with its implication of authority, lent a stabilizing influence to the surrounding area. Just the same, they were one long day's journey away, André noted. It would be well to keep a sharp watch. He took his robe and turned away toward the lookout post.

He tried not to look back or even notice as the girl stirred, murmured sleepily, and lifted the edge of her blanket to welcome her husband to its warmth.

7

>> >> >>

In the next few days of travel, André began to become better acquainted with his companions. He still avoided the girl, but he felt that he had chosen well when he picked Sergeant Cartier.

He was increasingly impressed with the sergeant's initiative and skill. The man seemed to take to the woods as a duck to water, becoming adept under the instruction of Brûle.

Brûle was another good man, André realized. The captain had chosen him well. He wondered how much Brûle knew about the mission. It did not seem to matter to the scout. He did his job well, a day at a time, educating the other two as he went.

Before they started, Brûle had made some strong suggestions as to weapons. Swords, he said, would be quite impractical. This had seemed reasonable, and both soldiers had agreed to match their weapons to their garments. Both were learning the use of the throwing ax. Both carried knives, slender fighting knives for quick use in time of need. André, of course, carried his match-less pistol.

Cartier had inquired of Brûle whether it might be practical to learn the use of the bow. The scout seemed pleased, and with his help, Cartier was rapidly mastering the weapon.

All had rejected the cumbersome matchlock muskets, with their fickle dependency on fair weather. Even a heavy fog had been known to make them useless, or at least no better than a club.

Cartier's progress with the bow was so spectacular that André decided to learn its skills too. The sergeant willingly lent his weapon, and the two practiced constantly when time permitted. Soon both were becoming proficient.

"It is good," observed Pale Star. "Either of you would do well in the Rabbit Society among my people."

"Rabbit Society?"

"Yes, Woodchuck. It is where our children are taught the skills of the warrior."

Brûle chuckled softly, leaving the soldiers to wonder whether Star's remark had actually been a compliment or not.

One evening when the two were alone, Cartier approached André in a confidential yet respectful manner.

"Lieutenant, would it be considered improper if I asked about the nature of your mission?"

Instantly, André assumed the defensive.

"Why do you ask, Sergeant?"

"Because no purpose has been stated. Lieutenant, it's plain this is no ordinary scouting trip. We're traveling fast, not stopping to scout. No one has said even where we're going, or how far."

"Yes, Sergeant, go on."

Now Cartier was uneasy, afraid he had gone too far.

"I'm sorry, sir, I should not have asked."

"No, no, Cartier. I chose you for this mission because I was confident you could be relied on. Tell me, what do you *think* is going on?"

"I don't know, sir. I didn't feel that Brûle would know more than I do. So you are the only one who knows. It must be a scout for a major push into the west. But, sir, with due respect, if anything happens to you, no one knows what we are to do."

It was a long speech for the sergeant. But André had to admit he was right. It would be a completely wasted mission if he, André, were incapacitated.

"You are right, Sergeant. I'd hoped to wait a little longer, but you all deserve to know what we're doing. We will discuss it tonight, we four."

Later, around the camp fire, he began the talk.

"Sergeant Cartier has convinced me today that we should all know our mission. This way, if anything happens to any of us, the others can take the word back. Now, Brûle, what has the captain told you?"

"Only that he wishes you to scout beyond the Big River, to the southwest."

"But I have seen that we travel mostly west," André observed.

There was just a flash of an uneasy glance between Brûle and his wife. Or could it have been imagination?

"Sir, we travel west to the Big River, then south by canoe, then west again."

"You have been there, Brûle?"

"No sir, only as far as the Big River. The captain said he wishes that we go beyond."

André nodded. This seemed a satisfactory explanation, and cleared up the puzzling matter of their present direction.

"Did the captain mention that we would go mostly by water?"

"Yes, Lieutenant. This I did not understand. Go where by water?"

"We are to look for a water passage to the southwest."

He saw no reason to tell more at this time, and planned to drop the matter. But Cartier was more astute than he realized.

"Begging the Lieutenant's pardon, sir, but the Water Passage—do they not say it is northwest?"

"They do, Sergeant. But 'they' have never found it. Perhaps because it is *not* northwest, but southwest?"

"*That* is our mission?"

"Why not, Sergeant? Is it not true that in this area the
streams all run that direction?"

"I do not know, sir. I am new to the area."

"Yes, it is true," injected Brûle. "They run into the Big
River, which also runs southwest."

"How many days to the Big River, Brûle?"

"Three, maybe four."

It was easy for André to become reinfected with the
excitement of discovery that had been evident in the
captain's office. In fact, he became almost expansive in
his description. Cartier, of course, could grasp the significance of the search, and the water route to the riches of
India.

Brûle was noncommittal. What mattered it to him, the
scout's attitude seemed to say, if one could paddle a
canoe to the other Big Salt Water or not? He said little,
only answered questions.

It was several days later before André realized that Pale
Star had seemed completely disinterested. During all of
the discussion the girl had said not one word at all.

André might have realized within a day or two that
something was wrong, except for the events of next morning. That was the day they were attacked.

8

>> >> >>

*A*pril the eighteenth day: Last night I have discussed
our mission with the rest of the party, and they share
my enthusiasm in the quest. We are to search for a
Southwest Waterway to the Western Sea, which will
lead to India. We are now about four days from the Big
River, which none of us have seen except Brûle and his
wife.

There was a disconcerting encounter this morning. We
were attacked by a group of natives, some of whom
carried matchlock guns of European make. We saw no
white men, and these weapons appear to be of a common type. They could have been obtained from either
our garrisons or the English.

We conducted ourselves well, killing three of the attackers and wounding another.

Brûle had cautioned the party as they set out that
morning. They were moving through country claimed by
several tribes with varying loyalties. The area, however,
was not totally controlled by anyone. Shifting power,

political intrigue, and varying policy by the whites who aspired to control created a constant state of turmoil.

The scout did not elaborate on the political details, but only warned of potential danger.

It was late morning, and they had traveled well. Brûle had passed word that they would stop soon at a watering place. André was beginning to anticipate the rest. His pack was still a tiresome burden, his muscles not yet accustomed to the stress.

They entered the clearing, the path widening and dividing to indicate a well-used stopping place or campground. To the right, more and greener grass and foliage suggested a water source. The travelers paused and began to unsling their packs.

Suddenly a man stepped from the bushes on the far side of the clearing. He held up a hand in the sign of peace and friendship, but André noted immediately that his left hand held a throwing-ax.

"Careful!" warned Brûle in French. André made ready to draw his pistol if necessary. It was already charged and primed.

"How are you called?" the scout signed.

The other man shook his head. He knew no sign-talk, or at least professed not to know.

This seemed odd, André thought. Tribes to the west used more sign-talk, rather than less. He was beginning to distrust this chance meeting. What was a lone man doing here, anyway, in an area that was recognized as dangerous? There must be others.

The party drew closer together, ready for the unexpected, while Brûle tried several languages and dialects. Finally they seemed to arrive at a mutually understandable tongue. The scout half-turned, with a broad smile, almost carelessly, as if translating welcome news. Yet when he spoke, his words, in French, were grim.

"I think he speaks no French," he said cheerfully, "so listen. There are others in the woods. I smell their matches, so they must mean to attack. Now, slowly take out weapons."

The others moved to do so. André drew his pistol and opened the pan, glancing down to see that it contained priming. From the corner of his eye, he saw Sergeant Cartier fit an arrow to his bowstring. Now he could plainly smell the acrid smoke of smoldering salpeter matches.

Brûle turned to continue the conversation with the stranger. Now his tones were crisp and commanding, and he used sign-talk as well. *Either he believes the other man understands*, thought André, *or he wants to let us know what is happening. Maybe both.*

"You lie!" Brûle accused. "Tell the others to come out!"

The man spread his hands in a helpless shrug, still smiling. But the bushes parted, and warriors slipped quietly into the clearing, fanning out left and right. André's military training let him quickly evaluate the situation. Seven men. Two carried guns, their matches lighted. He noted that neither had opened the pan yet. That would give them a moment or two.

It also implied that the others were not experts in the use of the weapons. Of the party facing them, those with the guns were probably least dangerous. Of the seven, the leader was probably the one to put down.

But danger also threatened from a man to the left. Lean and efficient-looking, the swarthy warrior kept moving at a crouch, circling like a stalking lobo wolf.

Brûle spoke softly in French, with apparently casual hand gestures.

"Star, the one on the left. Sky-Eyes, the leader is yours."

André tried to appear calm as he raised the pistol, but his heart was racing. The look of complete scorn on the face of the other man puzzled him for a moment. Then he realized that the man did not understand the pistol. Since there was no smoking match, the stranger assumed the weapon was not ready to fire!

With some degree of confidence now, André calmly sighted on a shell ornament that dangled at the chest of the other. He released the safety catch, secure in the fact his opponent must still shift the ax to his right hand before use.

He realized the truth almost too late. Like the swift

strike of a snake, the man's *left* hand rose and descended. The ax whirled forward.

The steel disc of the pistol was already spinning, but it seemed a long time before a spark reached the powder and the little gun boomed. The stranger threw up his hands as he was knocked backward to sprawl on the ground. André felt the whispering *swish* of his opponent's throwing-ax brush past his ear, and one of the matchlocks roared. Someone screamed, a cry of mortal terror.

André reached for his own ax, but the fight was over. The survivors of the attacking party scurried for cover.

One of the gun-carrying warriors lay transfixed by Cartier's arrow, his unfired musket beside him, match still smoking. Pale Star was retrieving her throwing-ax from the swarthy man's body to wipe it clean and replace it at her waist.

Apparently only Brûle's assailant had escaped, though bleeding heavily from an ax wound as he ran.

"Who are they?" André gasped.

"It does not matter, Sky-Eyes. Scalp hunters. They will not return."

Brûle moved forward to scalp the dead, deftly circling the hair and jerking the trophies free. He returned and extended a bloody offering to André.

"This left-hand thrower almost fooled me."

"Me, too," gulped André. "Brûle, you keep the scalp."

"It is good. Now we must move. We have far to go before dark, but first we rest at the spring ahead."

9
»» »» »»

Star watched her husband retrieve the scalps. He tucked the hair from her victim and that of the lieutenant in his belt. Hawk knew that she would not want the trophy. Among her people, far on the western prairie, scalping was unknown. She had been shocked when she saw the custom for the first time.

How long ago that seemed. She was only a child when she was stolen and carried off. She was fortunate to have been purchased later by Traveler and his wife, Plum Leaf. This couple had regarded her as the daughter they never had.

The period after the murder of her foster father was still a nightmare, but she thought less of it now. She had been married to Hawk for four winters now, since shortly after they had saved each other's lives from the madman Three Owls.

It was a good marriage. Star had become proud of her husband's skills. He was the most respected of scouts, and it was a great honor to be selected for this mission.

She had perfected many skills in her own right since

her marriage. Her ability with the throwing-ax rivaled even that of Hawk himself. It had proved fortunate today.

They had no children. She and Hawk had talked about that. Perhaps, they had concluded, it was because of the abuse she had suffered as a captive long ago, though she seemed normal enough now. At least, she felt that everything was good.

Except, of course, that she had always been a bit homesick. She wanted to return to the open grasslands and far horizons of her childhood. She and Hawk had talked of that, too. He had agreed someday to help her to go and visit her people, when the time was right. Now this appeared to be the time.

Perhaps it was fortunate, after all, that they were childless. It would have been very difficult to attempt this journey with small children.

One thing about this mission bothered her above all others, though. She found herself attracted strongly to the tall soldier, Sky-Eyes. Some women, she knew, would think nothing of such a feeling. Some would even devise some way to bed with him. But among the People, her upbringing had been strict. There were multiple marriages, but fidelity was expected. There were severe penalties for the unfaithful.

So deeply ingrained was this principle that even her attraction to Sky-Eyes made her feel guilty. There seemed little likelihood that she would ever have anything to feel guilty about. The lieutenant seemed almost unaware of her existence, at least as a woman.

What few contacts he had found necessary were carried out with a cold detachment. Even the sign-talk lessons were so cold, so impersonal. He had been quick, had grasped the thoughts behind the signs rapidly. But he had been seriously confined to the task at hand. There had been no suggestion of even mild flirtation. Then she had the guilty pang again, at the thought that there might have been. What a strange thing! She had never felt this way about anyone.

She had astonished herself by her reactions at the time of the skirmish. After she had determined that her own throw was true, she quickly turned to see how the others were faring. She had looked first for the lieutenant, and only then for her husband and the sergeant.

She was embarrassed, but none of the others seemed to notice. She managed to take pleasure in the skill that all had displayed in the crisis. It gave a great sense of security that each had accomplished what was required.

It was especially clever, of course, for Sky-Eyes to have seen through the treachery of a left-handed attacker who gave the friendship sign with his right hand while preparing to throw.

There was only a slight twinge of guilt when she thought this. She was able to convince herself that it was part of her pride in the success of the defense against superior numbers. Sky-Eyes had done well, but she had done well herself, as had Woodchuck and her husband. There was a degree of well-deserved pride in being part of an effective fighting team such as this.

Now she began to think ahead. In a few more sleeps they would arrive at the Big River, the village of White Squirrel. That chief had been a friend of her foster father. She wondered whether Squirrel was still alive. If so, he could help them. Of course, she reminded herself, it had been four winters. Much could happen in that time.

There had been much to jog her memory on this journey. She had identified the spot where Three Owls had killed and scalped his own cousin to take sole possession of her. She had said nothing, but the dread that she felt on that portion of the trail was a powerful thing. She actually stepped around the spot where she believed Winter Bear had fallen, to avoid disturbing his spirit.

There were bad memories for every camp site on the trail now. She could tell no one, not even her husband. She had traversed this trail in the other direction as a mistreated and sexually abused prisoner, little more than a child.

It would be better, she hoped, after they passed the spot where she had been captured and Traveler presumably killed.

She had not seen his dead body, and she had spent much time in wondering about the possibility that he was still alive. Probably not. Her captors had said that he was dead, and it seemed that in four years he would have found her or sent word.

No, she had given up the idea of his survival long ago. Her memories were just getting in the way of reality. She hoped that after they passed that place on the trail, the old ghosts could be laid to rest.

She thought long about all these things as she took her turn on guard that night. After she returned to her blanket she lay awake listening to the night sounds. Yes, she thought that she might feel better after they passed that grim spot.

It would be good to see White Squirrel again, too, if he still lived. He would remember her, and might know what happened to poor Traveler.

She finally drifted off to sleep, with one more troubled thought nagging at her fading consciousness. Why did the tall soldier whom she admired so much seem to dislike her so?

10

» » »

"Little Sister, is it really you?"

White Squirrel, a little older, a little fatter, and graying at the temples, welcomed the travelers into his village like long-lost relatives. Even Brûle was astonished.

"This is your husband, child?" The chief shook his head in wonder.

Star nodded.

"My chief, what do you know of Traveler?"

"I was about to ask you. We heard that he was killed, but no one seemed to know about a girl who had been with him."

"I was never really sure what happened to him. I did not see his body. They just told me."

"Who, little one?"

No one had called her that since she lost Traveler. With a pang of regret, she remembered how furious she used to become when he called her "little one." Now it sounded good to her. She swallowed hard.

"Three Owls and his cousin."

"Ah, those were bad ones. It is said Owls killed his own cousin?"

"Yes, Uncle. I saw it."

"Ah, it is bad. Then what happened to Three Owls? We heard he was killed by a woman at Mishi-ghan."

"By me. My husband and I killed him. Only, Hunting Hawk was not my husband then, of course."

"*You!*" White Squirrel's mouth dropped open in amazement.

"Yes, but that is long ago, Uncle. Now we are together. Let us enjoy."

"It is good. You will tell us stories tonight?"

Tales around the story-fires had been a big part of her life with Traveler. In meeting new tribes, the exchange of stories had been a favorite pastime, and she had become expert at it. She had had little opportunity in recent seasons.

"Of course, Uncle."

White Squirrel smiled, pleased.

"And where do you travel?"

"Southwest. Down the Big River."

The chief nodded.

"Come, you will stay in my lodge."

The welcome was almost overwhelming to Pale Star. She had almost overcome the seasons of not belonging, of being without family and friends in a strange land. The lost feeling was still there, however, just beneath the surface. She did not know how she could have survived without the calm assurance of Brûle.

She had been reluctant about the marriage at first. It required all her courage to trust any man. Brûle had been calm, patient, and nondemanding. Gradually, she had adjusted.

Still, underneath, she had never gotten over the loss of the prairie, the open country of her early years. There were still times when the woods and hills seemed to close in on her and stifle the life-breath in her chest. She would have an occasional wild impulse to run, to escape, to flee until the forests were behind and the free air of open country around her. She knew what it was. The rejuvenating spirit of the Sacred Hills of the People called to her.

Now, in this return to the village of White Squirrel,

the bittersweet memories of her journeys with Traveler came flooding back. She was reliving the times on the trail, both good and bad. There was a certain sad happiness in this place, in the security of friends.

It seemed to awaken the call of the prairie in her spirit, however. More than ever, she felt the call of the tallgrass hills of her home. And now, she was going home. Already, to the south of their trail, there had been occasional glimpses of open country and grasslands.

"My chief," she said to Squirrel as they walked through the village, "we will need canoes."

"Of course. The one you left here is old, though. We will find new ones."

"You still have Traveler's canoe?"

"Yes. I did not know when you might return. We have used it some."

"May I see it?"

The canoe was old, the bark shell dry and cracking, but it brought back many memories. Star ran her fingers over the painted eyes at the prow. Traveler had placed them there so the craft could see its way. And it had been good to them. They had escaped many dangers. Plum Leaf, her foster mother, had crossed over to the Spirit World cradled in the middle of this canoe on the bosom of the river.

"We will paint the eyes, like these, on the new canoes," she announced.

White Squirrel nodded in understanding.

"They are used by Traveler's people. Did you ever reach his tribe?"

"No. He was killed."

"It is bad. Traveler was my friend."

They returned to join the others, and Star was thinking of the story-fire tonight. She would tell the Creation story, of how the People came through a hollow log from inside the earth, summoned by the Old Man of the Shadows. Another favorite was always that of the bobcat's tail. Every tribe had a different story of that. Yes, it would be good, this story-session.

But then they must push on. Sky-Eyes was impatient

to search for the Water Passage. No less impatient, of course, than Star herself. She was going home.

She thought of the good fortune they had encountered, with White Squirrel eager to help with obtaining canoes. It would take a little time, she was aware, to teach the soldiers the necessary skills to go on. A day or two, at least. She and Brûle could teach them. Woodchuck seemed already to have some wilderness experience, and Sky-Eyes would learn quickly.

It would be best, she thought, for her and her husband to take the steering positions in the rear of each canoe. Then the inexperienced soldiers could more easily handle the prow.

From that assumption, it was only a quick realization that they must choose which man to pair with which. She had no desire to spend the next moon in a canoe with Sky-Eyes. It was already apparent that he disliked her. He was still avoiding her at all costs. Their only contact was in the learning of the sign-talk. He was very good at that, but did not allow for more than the most brief of conversations otherwise.

No, it would never do for them to work day after day in the same canoe. Sky-Eyes would come to resent her even more, though she still did not know why. It was no matter. She would be much more comfortable working with Woodchuck. The sergeant was quiet and efficient, comfortable to be around. He would be good to work with.

Besides, Star had to admit, with some irritation at herself, she still felt an attraction to the tall lieutenant. While they traveled on the trail, he was out of sight part of the time. In a canoe, day after day on the river, it would be different. If he were her partner, she would be looking at his back. She did not think it would be good to be constantly aware of the breadth of his shoulders, the curl of hair at the back of his neck, and the smooth ripple of his muscles at each stroke of the paddle.

Irritably, she shook her head to clear it of such thoughts, and occupied herself with other things.

11

>> >> >>

May, the twenty-seventh day: Tomorrow we start
down the stream which local natives call the Big River.
Their legends are quite sketchy, but there are suggestions that it runs into a "Big Salty Water" a great distance
from here. This seems favorable to our mission.

Both Sgt. Cartier and I are becoming proficient in the
hand-sign talk. It appears that it is used even more in
the regions to the west. We are also learning to use the
native boats, which will be our primary transportation
from this point. We will take two of these canoes.

"You will take the front in my canoe, Lieutenant,"
Brûle announced. "Sergeant Cartier will go in the other
with my wife."

He did not state the reason, that Pale Star had requested it so.

André thought nothing of it either. He was grateful
that he would not be in the same canoe as the girl. That
would be almost more than he could tolerate. He was

becoming increasingly aware of her. Her beauty and grace
of motion set her above and apart from any woman he
had ever seen.

As if that were not enough, her keen, quiet judgment
became constantly more apparent. André had been impressed by the respect shown her in this village. The
chief and his people had welcomed her eagerly, and
requested story-fire tales.

That, too, had been impressive. The girl was a natural
storyteller, using wit and wisdom to keep the listener spellbound. She announced to begin with that she was somewhat
inexperienced in the languages of the listeners. She would
use a combination of tongues, as well as sign-talk.

This pleased the lieutenant greatly. It would allow
him to follow the story. It did not fail to impress him
that Pale Star was skilled in languages. Some people
were gifted in this way. He recalled similar situations in
his own country. A person growing up in the border
towns might often be called upon to understand several
languages besides his own. It had never occurred to him
that a similar situation might occur among the nations
of the New World.

Now he sat with other listeners around a story-fire in
the wilderness, chuckling with people of different tribes
and cultures. All could enjoy the story of the bobcat's
tail, lost through a knothole in a tree.

But the real thrill was to watch the storyteller as she
manipulated the crowd. She used, apparently, several
local tongues, throwing in a phrase here and there that
delighted certain fragments of her mixed audience. She
even used a few words of French occasionally to remind
the soldiers that she had not forgotten them.

This was truly a remarkable woman. One could almost say brilliant. In his mind's eye he could see her in
Paris, dressed in the latest of fashion, charming the no-
bility with quick witticisms and sparkling conversation.

André shook his head in disbelief at such thoughts. He
must try harder to rid his mind of the spell of this, the
most intriguing of women.

Close by his disturbing feelings for Pale Star was his
increasing respect and admiration for her husband. Brûle

was in all respects a man's man. He could be counted on.
He was quick to think, to make decisions, and to act on
them. André had only to think back on the skirmish in
the woods to see that. The scout had calmly set the stage
and helped the little party defeat a superior force. He
had taken none of the credit, but had praised the others
in the party. This was the sort of man to be allied with
in time of emergency, a born leader.

The feeling of respect seemed to be mutual, too. André
felt that the scout was pleased with his performance in
the skirmish. It had been close, the trick of the thrown
ax from the left hand. He had barely managed to throw
the shot that killed the leader of the attackers. And for
this he had received the quiet approval of the scout.

"You have done well, Sky-Eyes."

André was a little startled at his own reaction. Here
was a man, actually a subordinate, praising a superior
officer. And Lieutenant André Du Pres was pleased to be
commended in this fashion. There was no impertinence
in the remark, merely respect, and it was taken as such.

All of this had the effect of making it more difficult to
deal with the feelings he had for this man's wife. He
must at all costs resist these feelings. He thought again
of the Calvinists and their insistence that man is by
nature evil. He could believe that his feelings for his
friend's wife were evil. Why, then, did they seem so
right? It would be so much easier somehow if the husband of Pale Star were cruel or incompetent or unreliable.

"Now, place your weight exactly in the middle," Brûle
was saying. "Right. Now move forward."

On the first few tries the canoe wobbled alarmingly.
André could see that Sergeant Cartier was having much
better luck. The sergeant had been on the frontier longer
and must have had some experience with the craft.

It was embarrassing to be the commanding officer of
the party and have less expertise than any of the others.

"Relax," Brûle was saying. "Let your body move with
the motion of the canoe. There, that is better. Keep low."

At no time did the scout seem to talk down to him,
André noted. There was respect and encouragement, but
no disdain.

He soon discovered that it was all a matter of balance, which was learned fairly rapidly.

"Good," encouraged Brûle, "it comes quickly. Let us cross the river and back."

With confidence came ability, and in a few sorties on the river the progress of the student became apparent.

"It goes well," announced the scout as they beached the canoes at sunset. "Tomorrow we will practice with loaded canoes, and the day after, start downriver."

André was elated. It seemed to him that an important phase of the expedition was behind: If only the rest would proceed as well.

And if only, he reminded himself as an afterthought, he could manage to refrain from damaging the expedition by coveting his friend's wife.

12
>> >> >>

The two canoes slid across the surface noiselessly, with scarcely a ripple behind. They traveled with the current of the river, at times requiring no paddling at all, beyond the occasional move of the steersman in the rear of each craft.

In the prow of the canoe he shared with Brûle, André Du Pres stared in wonder at the new sights and sounds. Part of his task was to observe closely for snags and obstacles in the river. At this, he had done well. But there were long stretches of smooth water, where he could relax and watch the land slip past as they traveled.

He was astonished at the geography of the country. The river itself, of course, was rather remarkable. It was, at this point, as wide as the rivers of his native country. Each day they passed the mouths of unnamed streams that added to its size. André was just beginning to comprehend the possible enormity of the Big River by the time it crossed the continent. Its width could be beyond belief at its mouth.

He tried to recall the shape of the western shoreline on

the map in Captain Le Blanc's office. Had there not been a bay, a long narrow inlet, with a river at its head? Yes, he was certain. Le Blanc had pointed to a river, charted only a short distance inland. If that was this same river, its mouth might be the bay indicated on the crude map. He longed for another glance at the map.

"Beaver."

Brûle spoke the single word and pointed with his paddle. On the western shore, it appeared that someone had been cutting timber. There were bright fresh tree stumps here and there and a tangle of downed trees. The scout casually dipped his paddle, and the canoe responded by a gentle turn in that direction. André could now see an animal swimming in the water, and another on the shore. The activity appeared to be around the mouth of a small stream that meandered to join the river at this point.

"Many beaver!" Brûle spoke again.

The scout sounded almost excited, his voice tense.

"Good trapping!"

Slowly, André began to realize that the territory they were seeing was virgin wilderness. The beaver here had never been trapped, because the westward push had not reached this point yet. It gave him a strange, primitive feeling. It was almost like being present at Creation. He could feel a spiritual pull, almost a religious experience as he gazed across the new land.

His reverie was disturbed by a loud slapping splash as a beaver dived and gave warning to the others as it disappeared. André was startled, as always, by the performance. He had observed beavers before. The creatures would be moving quietly, undisturbed, and then suddenly one would take alarm and slap the water with its flat tail. Instantly, all would disappear. There was no questioning the alarm signal. It was amazing to him, this discipline that existed among these lesser creatures.

Brûle dipped his paddle again and then moved on. They had seen beaver three times in the past two days, and André was making a mental note. This would be a rich area for fur trapping when his people pushed this far.

He relaxed again and looked beyond the fringe of trees along the western bank. Here was perhaps the most spectacular impression of all he had encountered on this journey so far. He had been entirely unprepared for the vastness of the grassland.

Such a short distance away, only a few weeks' travel, Fort Mishi-ghan had been in a forested area. He had been vaguely aware that there were grassland areas to the south. On the first leg of their journey, the overland trek had been characterized by glimpses of prairie.

It was almost as if, at times, they had traveled along a dividing line. To their right as they walked had been forest; to their left, open country.

Still, nothing had prepared him for the enormity of what he now saw. Along the Big River, and along the water courses that joined it from time to time, were trees. Many were the soft, fast-growing willows, but others were veritable giants. It had taken André some time to realize the size of some of these monarchs. He had finally begun to understand that his perspective was distorted. Seen against the hugeness of the prairie, the magnificent blue bowl of the sky, and the width of the great river, individual trees were dwarfed by comparison.

It did not fully come home to him until they stopped on a sandbar one night and out of curiosity he measured a giant cottonwood on the shore. By means of comparison, using his own height to mark a known measure on the trunk, he estimated the tree's height. At first he was certain he had miscalculated, and repeated the whole procedure. But no, it was correct. The great sentinel at the river's bend was actually thirteen times his own height, or nearly eighty feet tall.

By spanning the trunk with his arms, he completed the exercise, and was even more astonished. Extending his arms as widely as he could, he marked with the tip of his reaching fingers. He found that four spans of his arms would barely encompass the trunk of the tree. Moreover, he could see other specimens up and down the river that appeared even larger.

This puzzled the young lieutenant. Why, if this area was so rich and fertile as to produce these giant trees, was the entire area not forested? Instead, there was grass as far as eye could see, except at the watercourses. Only an ocasional brushy draw or a lone cottonwood in an open area gave exception.

"Brûle, why is it that trees do not grow in the grassland?"

The scout shrugged.

"I do not know. Ask Star. She is of the prairie."

The girl, who overheard, hardly looked up. She did not wait for the question, but gave a terse, one-word answer.

"Fire."

"Fire?"

"Yes, Sky-Eyes. They burn the grass."

"Who?"

"The people. Those who live there."

André did not understand at all, but was reluctant to continue the conversation. Conversations with the girl were becoming increasingly difficult, anyway. In addition to his own feelings, he had noticed a growing coolness on her part. When it was necessary to speak to him at all, her comments were quick and concise. For some reason unknown to him, he realized, she disliked him more and more.

That, he conceded, might make things better. Yes, it would be better if their interactions were cold and impersonal. It might avoid many problems, and much trouble.

Somehow, as much as he rationalized along these lines, it did not seem to make it any easier.

13

» » »

May, the third day: We have traveled on the River for some distance now. The direction of flow is southwest, This is an immense grassland, with great trees along the watercourses. There are many beaver and otter, the area untrapped as yet. We have seen no natives.

There was a severe storm last night, its strength in proportion to the vastness that is this land.

André paused, almost embarrassed that he had become so flowery in his description. But no, this land deserved such words. It was impossible to describe in lesser terms. He rewrapped the journal and stowed the packet in his buckskin pocket.

For that matter, it was impossible to describe at all. A person would have to experience it, the far reach of the horizons, the broad expanse of the great sky. One could see forever, it seemed.

Yet, when the sun sank in the evening, it seemed almost close enough to touch. There was a sense of omnipotence, a feeling of power at being part of such a gigantic panorama.

Somehow, at the same time, there was a feeling of humility, of smallness. It was only in being a part of the whole that the observer could gain the feeling of mastery.

How odd, he thought, that he should be thinking along these lines. He had almost attempted to include this feeling in his journal. But no reader of his pages could possibly understand without the experience. He would attempt to keep this a factual military report, ignoring the emotions that the land was beginning to evoke. He would report their progress, the prevalence of beaver and otter and other furbearers. He would mention the buffalo that were beginning to be seen in more abundance.

But he would avoid attempts at explaining his feelings. He would also try to avoid explaining, even to himself, why his feeling for the land kept becoming confused with his feeling for the tall, beautiful woman who was the wife of his friend.

He could hardly bear the thought of her sharing the blankets with Brûle during the chill of the cool spring nights. Then he was irritated at this thought and shook it angrily from his head.

Yet when he looked over the prairie at a spectacular sunset or watched the moon rise to spread liquid silver across the grassland, he thought of the girl. Her spirit had become one with that of the plains in his mind. Just as he was falling in love with the quiet beauty of the ever-changing grassland, he found himself falling more deeply in love with Pale Star. He could not help it, any more than the coyote on the hill could help crying to the moon.

The storm they encountered on the river was a thrilling and somewhat frightening experience. It was midday, and the sky had been a deep, cloudless blue as they traveled that morning. The first inkling was a low cloud bank in the northwest.

André thought at first that he was looking at a range of undiscovered mountains, blue with the haze of distance. He wondered if the course of their travel on the river would bring them closer, but it appeared not. It was not long, however, until he realized that the dark blue-gray mass on the horizon was a layer of storm clouds.

The mass rose and expanded, almost perceptible in its mushroomlike growth. Now its expanse covered the entire western horizon. From the center of the cloud bank rose towering columns of dazzling-white thunderheads, growing and covering the western sky.

André had never seen anything like this before. He realized that the ability to watch the storm's progress from such a vast distance was altering his perspective. It was similar, he recalled, to watching the approach of a storm at sea. That had been a fearsome thing during the ship's crossing.

This, somehow, was more exciting to him. Where the storm at sea had involved wind and water, this was a different feeling. He could observe with an air of detachment almost. The earth where the river flowed was calm, without even a breeze, yet he could see the churning in the distant clouds. It all added to the feeling he had felt before, the sensation of godlike omnipotence that came with being part of this enormous panorama of earth and sky.

Now the travelers could see flashes of orange fire flickering in the dirty gray of the storm's lower cloud bank. Occasionally, there was a low mutter of thunder, poorly heard in the distance.

Brûle paused and waited for the other canoe to come alongside. He spoke to his wife questioningly.

"Rain-Maker tunes his drum," she answered in French so that the others might understand. "We should camp."

They turned toward the eastern bank of the river and cruised quietly, looking for a camp site.

"There!" Brûle pointed.

They beached the canoes and carried them some distance up the sloping shore. Supplies and packs were piled beneath the overturned canoes, and they turned to watch the storm approach. André thought with some degree of awe that they had watched the approaching cloud bank travel across an expanse of prairie that would require many days for people to traverse.

They had stopped none too soon. The flicker of lightning was almost constant now, and the soft mutter of thunder became an ominous rumble. The sun was obscured by the roll of the towering thunderheads. Still, the area where they sat was quiet and still.

André moved to a point where he could watch the advancing front. How very like an army on the march, he thought. He could see the blur of falling rain in the distance, creeping rapidly over the plain. Behind the front, nothing could be seen.

The thunder was closer now, bolts of lightning stabbing at the earth along the storm's leading edge. Still, the front was so far away that there was a long pause between the fire's flash and the sound of the booming thunder.

It came closer, while André stared in fascination. Now the tops of trees along the opposite bank of the river began to stir with a restless discontent. One giant cottonwood shuddered under the blow of a lightning bolt, causing André to wince involuntarily.

"The spirit of the cottonwood attracts real-fire," observed Pale Star.

André would have liked to ask more about this curious statement, but the storm swept out into the river. Trees churned and twisted in the wind and the next moment were obscured from view by driving rain. They could see the advance of the rain across the broad water. The relatively quiet flow of the river's surface was whipped to a blur of froth by the beating of falling rain and wind.

The storm swept across the river toward them. At the last moment, the travelers retreated to crouch beneath the canoes while the world disappeared in a wet gray-blue and the wind and thunder roared around them.

Before nightfall the storm had cleared. They could crawl from the shelter of the canoes to stand in a clean-washed world and watch the brilliance of a prairie sunset. In sharp contrast to the violence just past, the quiet melody of a bird song floated in the evening twilight.

"We stay here," decided Brûle abruptly.

The camp site had been chosen for a dual purpose, shelter from the storm and a place for the night. The scout drew an armful of dry kindling from beneath one of the canoes and soon had a fire crackling. The fire was pleasant, since the storm had chilled the evening sharply. The warmth of their blankets would be good tonight.

André tried to ignore the next thought, which followed that of warmth and blankets.

14

» » »

André stood looking at the sky for a long time. He
had come to the habit of doing so. For one thing, there
was more sky to look at. Then the quality of this sky
was different, the blue-black of its velvet spangled with
innumerable stars. The stars had never seemed so close
before.

He had begun what now was almost a nightly ritual
out of sheer enjoyment. He would watch the sky and
listen to the call of coyotes for a little while before
retiring. Occasionally he would hear the deeper cry of a
hunting wolf or the distant bellow of a buffalo bull.

Now André's monitoring of the night sky had taken on
a new meaning. He was troubled over something. He had
questioned his observations at first, but there was no
doubt. Something was wrong.

When they had started the water portion of the journey, the basic flow of the river had been almost directly
southwest. That had been an excellent sign for his mission. There had been some deviation, naturally, in the

river's wandering course, but there was no doubt about
the general direction.

It was shortly after the storm that he began to notice
the change. Or rather, not to notice. His first inkling that
something was wrong came after two days of winding
and turning of the river's course. André had lost his basic
sense of direction, and sought to reorient himself that
night.

He easily located the constellation of Ursa Major and
aligned the two stars to point to the polestar in the
north. It was not exactly where he had expected, but
somewhat farther to the right. The wandering direction
of the past two days had confused him. Just to make
certain, he re-identified the constellation and aligned to
the polestar again. Yes, it was correct. The thought crossed
his mind that perhaps there was some undiscovered vari-
ation at this latitude. But no, he had been taught at the
académie that the polestar is constant in position. Surely
he had become more confused than he realized over the
twisting course of the past two days.

Now he began to take special note each night of any
change in direction. Each night, the stars verified his
impression. The general direction of their travel had
changed. Although they had started toward the southwest, it now appeared that the river was following a
generally southern direction.

Ah, well, it was no matter, he decided. No river runs
straight. In a day or two, its course might be southwest,
even west for a time.

But he continued to watch, and to read the polestar. In
the back of his journal, he was sketching a crude map,
attempting to log the direction of travel each day or two.

Now almost a fortnight had passed since the storm,
and there had been no major shift in direction. The
course of the river was almost due south, perhaps even a
bit *east* of south. André was troubled, and a little puzzled. Why did the others not notice the discrepancy?

At first he approached Cartier.

"Sergeant, have you noticed any change in our direction?"

"No, sir. The river winds somewhat. Why, is there a
problem, Lieutenant?"

"No, probably not. You are right, the river wanders."

So, he thought to himself. He has not noticed. He would ask the scout.

"Brûle, it seems we are no longer traveling southwest, but due south. Is this right?"

Brûle looked at him a long time, glanced at the stars for a moment, and finally shrugged. Apparently this had not occurred to him either.

"I do not know, Sky-Eyes. Unless we leave the river, we follow where it goes, no?"

It was a logical answer, but did not satisfy André. If Captain Le Blanc's theory was correct, they must travel a long distance to the west before encountering the Pacific. This southern direction seemed wrong.

"Does the river run west below where we are now?"

Brûle shrugged again.

"I do not know. I will ask my wife."

Of course, André recalled. She has been here before. He had hesitated to bring her into the conversation, but she could contribute the answer. He must suppress the ever-stronger feeling for her and think of the success of the expedition.

"Star, come here," Brûle called.

The girl glided around the fire and approached to sit near the men.

"Sky-Eyes wants to know of the river's course below here."

She turned her gaze on the lieutenant. The fire high-lighted her shining hair and reflected flickering sparks from dark eyes. André had never seen her more beautiful.

"Yes, Sky-Eyes? What did you wish to know?"

"We seem to be traveling south, not southwest. Does the river turn west again?"

"Of course. Rivers do not travel a straight path."

"Yes, I know. But we travel south for many sleeps now."

The girl stared at him, and André felt that he would believe the sun rises in the west if she told him so.

"Sky-Eyes," she said, now dropping her gaze, "we can only follow the river, unless we walk."

André nodded. That was essentially what her husband

had said. It was true, of course, but he was still uneasy.
Something was not quite right here. The girl was shutting
him out, failing to give him information that he needed.
If only she did not dislike him so. She seemed to become
more distant and aloof every day.

He tried another approach.

"Star, tell me what is ahead. How are the rivers of your
country?"

She seemed to relent.

"What do you wish to know?"

"Does this Big River cross the country of your people?"

"There is a Big River. It passes to the north of our
country."

"It runs east and west? Is it this same river?"

"Sky-Eyes, you must know that I did not leave my
own land by river. We traveled far to the east, overland,
before I was stolen."

He had not known that.

"Then how did you get to Mishi-ghan?"

"Traveled north by land until we struck the Big River,
this river."

André was euphoric, excited beyond belief. This seemed
to verify the theory. A "big river" running east and west
to the north of Star's country. As a child, she had traveled far to the east, then north, and had finally come to
this river, on which they now traveled. It all seemed to
fit.

"How long before the river turns west again?"

"I do not know, Sky-Eyes. I did not come this way."

André did not notice the flaw in her story. If she had
traveled north until she reached an east-west river and
followed upstream, this would be a portion of the river
she had traveled. He was too excited to think clearly.

15

》》 》》 》》

Pale Star lay in the warmth of her blankets and stared at the night sky. Beside her, the soft breathing of Hunting Hawk told of restful slumber. Woodchuck was on guard, and across the fire, the blanketed form of Sky-Eyes lay unmoving.

Her deception must soon come to an end. She had been uncomfortable from the first, to mislead them all in this way.

Actually, she had not originally intended to mislead. She had told her husband, from the time they met, that someday she would go home. That had not seemed to bother him. This assignment appeared to be a great opportunity for him, a chance to make his skill known.

Hunting Hawk, or "Brûle," as he was known to the soldiers, was skilled, of course. Star took pride in the fact that her man was the finest of the scouts. She also knew that he had never been beyond the Big River.

While she had not actually told any untruths, she had let it appear that she thought the mission reasonable. By not telling all she knew of the land to the west, she had

63

misled the others. This she regretted somewhat, but her goal was important, that of returning to her people.

Hawk knew her feelings, and had let her direct the mission since they had arrived at the Big River. Actually, there had been few choices. They traveled on the river, with no alternative. Since they sought a water passage, it was of no use to leave the river. No one had been the wiser as they traveled.

No one, that is, until recently. Sky-Eyes had become suspicious. He was waiting for the Big River to turn west. She was impressed once more with his intelligence and quickness. She was sorry that it had been necessary to mislead him. In his excitement over the mission, he had overlooked her obvious lie, that of not having been on this portion of the river before.

Hunting Hawk had noticed.

"Why did you lie to Sky-Eyes?" he had asked later.

She had always been truthful to her husband, and she would do so now. She looked straight into his eyes.

"Because I am going home."

"I am made to understand."

"Will you tell him?" she asked.

"Not yet. Sometime, you must."

"Yes. But not now. Thank you, Hawk."

"It is nothing. You are my wife."

"Yes."

Then why, her thoughts kept nagging at her, why do I still feel the attraction to Sky-Eyes?

It was good that he had such an intense dislike for her, she knew. Otherwise, it would be even harder. He could hardly bring himself to question her about the river the other evening. That had made it easier to lie to him.

What made it harder was that she had seen him grow in spirit the farther they progressed into the grassland. She did not see the same change in her husband.

Hawk was a creature of the forests and seemed to have an oppressed feeling for the wide sky that was her home. Sky-Eyes, on the contrary, had seemed to revel in the far horizons. For a time she had thought it strange that someone from a far distant land across the Salty Water would feel the spirit of the prairie. But Sky-Eyes did. She could tell. There was a blending of his spirit with that of the land that was unmistakable. To a lesser degree, she felt it in Woodchuck. But he was a trifle slower, less intense, than the lieutenant.

In her husband, there seemed to be little or none of this spirit-feeling at all. She was sorry for this, because she would have liked to share. She would have liked to share her thoughts with Sky-Eyes, even, but that could never be.

All this spirit-feeling, of course, made it even more difficult to plan the necessary deceptions of upcoming days. She had kept even from her husband the fact that the mission was coming to a climax.

It could not be more than a few days until they passed the mouth of the Big River of her people. It would be good to travel upstream by canoe on that river, to approach her own land more closely. But she could not convince Sky-Eyes that it would be right to go *up* the stream. It would prove her lie.

She could, of course, steal one of the canoes and go upstream alone, but she had already rejected such a plan. It would place the others at risk, with only one canoe.

No, she must try to conceal the existence of the river's mouth, if possible, and if not, to explain it away. She could say that the Big River turns west beyond this junction.

Anyway, they must *pass* the river's mouth and then she must leave them. Star had thought long and hard about this. Hawk would understand her need. She would gladly take him with her. He might consent to go, even, but she could not ask him to make such a decision. He should not have to decide between her and his loyalty to the soldiers.

So, she would relieve him of that decision. He would mourn her loss, she was sure, but he would recover. The men might wait and search for a day or two, but then they would leave the area.

She did not try to guess whether Hawk would take them back or continue on down the river. Surely he knew their quest was useless. It was no matter.

As soon as a chance offered, after they passed the

mouth of the other Big River, she would be gone. It was a long trip overland, but she saw no other way. She would take a few supplies and travel light and fast.

She would miss her husband, of course, but she had never concealed her wish to do this. Hawk would not be surprised, after he thought about it a little. She might even go back to him later.

Star wondered a little what Sky-Eyes would think of her. She was sorry that his mission would fail. It would have failed anyway, but she need not have let it come this far. It was simply that it must come this far and then fail, to provide her a way home.

She hoped that he would not hate her too much more than she already did.

16

>> >> >>

The time had come. Pale Star had worried for many days about how she would lead the party past the junction of the two rivers. She had begun to recognize landmarks, dimly remembered from her journey upstream as a captive five years earlier. At that time she had memorized every rocky outcrop, every twist and turn of the mighty river, every distinctively shaped tree.

There had been doubt in her mind that she could still remember. During her original journey, she had thought from day to day in terms of escape. Her observations, she had thought, were to be used within days, or weeks at the most.

Now, five years later, it was gratifying to find that she still remembered. Within a day's travel, they would pass the junction of the rivers. A large stream which she believed to be the Big River of her people emptied into the Big River on which they traveled.

She still felt that it might be necessary to explain away

that stream. At the point of junction, the smaller of the two was flowing from the northwest. Surely she could make the others believe that it was somewhere below this point that the combined Big River turned its course westward.

Then, once beyond the junction, she would slip away as soon as opportunity offered, probably at the first night camp. Already, she had tied a small packet of supplies together and hidden it in her blanket.

The weather had favored her plan. Now, a day from the river's junction, a change had occurred. They woke to a misty world of fog and damp. Clouds hung low along the stream and mingled with the smoky tendrils of mist that rose from the surface of the water. Sounds were muffled, and curiously, magnified at the same time. The raucous cry that she recognized as that of a little green heron rattled through the fog. The bird could have been a few steps away or a few bow-shots. Distance was distorted.

"Can we travel in this?" asked Sky-Eyes.

"Oh yes," answered Star quickly. "The river is wide. We will stay in the main current."

Hunting Hawk looked at her strangely, but said nothing.

"The fog will soon lift," she continued.

"Maybe we should wait?"

"No, Sky-Eyes. It will go well."

She was hoping that the fog would not lift, that they could travel past the river junction while the others were unable to see their surroundings. That would make it easy, and she would have no convincing to do, no deception.

The day seemed favorable to her purpose, the clouds and fog covering the whole world. It was completely unlike the thunderstorm they had encountered earlier.

Star reasoned that if they pushed along through the day, it would be late afternoon when they passed the river junction. If they had not reached it by then, she would suggest a stop for the night, and hope that the next morning would be foggy too.

Actually, she realized, they should not have been traveling. They could see a very little distance ahead. All day, a fine mist gathered and clung in droplets on their hands and faces, their hair, and their buckskins. Even in this, the Moon of Growing, the dampness became an uncomfortable chill. No one, it seemed, was willing to be the first to complain, so no one spoke.

From time to time, Star realized that her husband was looking at her strangely. Even if the others did not know that something was not as it should be, she could tell that Hawk knew. He was willing to support her in her plan, no matter what it might be. Her heart went out to him, and with pangs of guilt she regretted the need to wrong him. A time or two, her resolve almost weakened.

In late afternoon, the mist thickened to a light drizzle and became even more uncomfortable.

"Shall we stop now?" Hawk called to the dimly seen other canoe.

"Soon!" she answered.

They were approaching the spot where she believed the junction to be, and they must not stop there for the night. Her entire deception might be exposed. Day was beginning to darken early because of the overcast, and conditions seemed favorable to slip past the other river's mouth before they camped.

Now Star thought she could see the opening in the trees along the shore. A broad expanse of water replaced the ragged fringe of timber to their right. She feared that the others would notice too, but a quick glance showed only lowered heads and hunched shoulders against the chill of the damp drizzle.

A patch of fog drifted across her field of vision, obscuring the river's mouth. Good. They would be past in a short while. She dipped her paddle strongly.

It was at about that time that she realized that something was wrong. There was a subtle change in the feel of the water against the canoe. It was a tremor, almost a shudder that she felt, and the craft dipped and rocked.

A tangle of brush and dead sticks floated past on her right, and she pushed it away with her paddle. What was happening? There should be no debris in a stream's center unless it was rising rapidly. In normal times, such flotsam found its way into back-eddies along the shore.

Then the truth flashed through her mind. She had been so preoccupied with her plan that she had been very foolish. The river on which they traveled was behaving normally, but she had no knowledge of the condition of the stream flowing into it. Rains upstream, to the northwest, could have caused it to rise.

Star had made a serious error in judgment. In her eagerness to escape to her people, she had led the party into grave danger without realizing it. Another raft of weeds and driftwood swept past. The canoe was still rocking and tossing along the rough surface as the two rivers mixed and mingled.

"What is it?" Hawk called from the unseen canoe at her left.

"Hawk!" she yelled. "There is another stream, in flood! Pull for shore!"

Her plans, her deceptions were destroyed, forgotten in the more destructive threat of the flood. It was now a matter of survival. If, she reminded herself, it was not already too late.

Ahead and to her right, trees loomed in the dim fog. They must be nearly past the junction.

"Woodchuck," she called to the sergeant in the prow of her canoe, "we head for those trees. Pull, now."

They were caught in the force of the river's current, pushed rapidly downstream. From the corner of her eye, she saw the other canoe approach from the left. The paddlers were fighting, pulling, trying to cross the swirling flood to reach the west bank. The first clump of trees swept past and was left behind, but now they were gaining, approaching the shore.

It seemed, though, that the flood was pushing even harder, throwing them downstream at an alarming rate. Star felt that they had no control whatever. They were merely another speck of drift, being sucked into the stream's center on the rising flood. They *must* reach shore.

"Now! Harder!" she called, and the canoe responded to their strokes. The shore was nearer now.

Her entire attention was fastened on the trees and the bank. Otherwise, she would never have failed to see the dead snag in the river ahead. She was completely unaware until she heard Woodchuck's warning yell, and a heartbeat later felt the jagged limbs tear into the underbelly of the canoe.

17

» » »

André had suffered through the damp, miserable day, puzzled as to the reason. Brûle and his wife had, until today, seemed cautious in their planning. The party took no unnecessary risks.

He had noticed that now the girl seemed to be making more of the decisions. It was not an overt thing. She would confer with her husband in private, and then the scout would inform the others of their course of action.

At first this had not seemed unusual. After all, Brûle had openly admitted from the first that he had not been farther west than the Big River. They were moving into the plains, the native home of Pale Star's people.

An unanswered question nagged at the back of the lieutenant's mind, however. Star had plainly stated that she had never been on this section of the river before. If this was true, the travelers would all have equal unfamiliarity with their watery trail. Brûle, as scout, would be the logical one to make decisions as to travel, rest, and camp sites.

Instead, the scout was apparently taking less initiative,

allowing his wife to direct the decision-making. André could see that it was logical, in a way. This was her country that they were approaching. Perhaps she *should* be the one making the decisions.

Then again, only a few days ago, she had disclaimed knowledge of this part of the river. This made him uneasy.

His doubts grew during the day as they traveled in the damp fog. It would have seemed more logical to camp for a day or two until the fog lifted and the light intermittent drizzle became less of a problem. He saw no reason to push ahead into an unknown region without even being able to see.

Water gathered in droplets on his hair and trickled between his shoulder blades. It was an uncomfortable sensation, like the tickle of a crawling insect inside his clothing.

Besides, he was chilly. The damp of the fog seemed to drift right through flesh and bone. The air felt cold, in contrast to the warmth of the water. His hand occasionally touched the surface as he paddled, and the water's warm sensation was surprising, almost pleasant.

André did not know exactly when the change occurred. He was paddling with the current, paying little attention to anything except the interminable day and the seemingly endless river. The other canoe was somewhere to their right, unseen in the fog at the moment.

He became aware of a different feel in the current, in the way the canoe rode the surface. There was a tremor or thrill that seemed to touch the sensitive shell of the craft.

Brûle seemed to notice too.

"What is it?" the scout called through the fog.

André could not hear all of the girl's answer. He only caught the urgent message that they must pull for the shore. He dipped his paddle strongly.

The canoe must be kept aligned with the current. A push from the side would make the craft unmanageable and might even capsize it by causing it to roll.

Now, through the fog, he could dimly see the outline of the other canoe. In the prow, Sergeant Cartier pulled strongly, while Star tried to maneuver.

André saw the danger before the others. At first he had the impression of a gigantic water creature rising from the depths to attack. Then he realized that it was a tree, uprooted long ago, probably. Now broken and thoroughly waterlogged, such a fallen giant would lie for months or years in a forgotten back-eddy of the river.

Now, with the flood mobilizing all sorts of drift, the great tree was moving. He could see the slow rolling motion as it tumbled along with the current. Broken snags poked their tips above water, to disappear again with the roll of the moving timber.

All of this flashed instantaneously through his mind. Both canoes were being sucked forward by the flood, to thrust against the jagged obstacle.

The other canoe struck first. He caught a glimpse of a broken limb as it thrust up between the two paddlers. The sergeant was thrown forward violently, to land among the churning snags. He was dragged under almost instantly.

Pale Star managed to throw herself clear. André saw her strike the water, submerge, and come to the surface again, fighting to stay afloat. A moment later he was fighting for his own life.

He felt the shudder as a jagged limb ripped into the canoe, and a second impact as it rose behind him. There was a muffled cry from Brûle. André tried to glance behind him, but before he could see anything, he caught a glimpse of motion from his right.

He tried to dodge, but the jagged stub caught him across the shoulder. The canoe was being pulled under, impaled and trapped. He threw himself into the water, fighting to stay free of the rolling tangle.

"Over here! This way!" yelled the frantic voice of Pale Star.

He attempted to swim in that direction, but was swept along by the current. Again, for a moment, he felt that the river and the tree were living things, trying to destroy him. He fought back.

He could see the figure of the girl ahead of him now. He eluded the undertow of a whirling eddy and struggled toward her.

André did not even see the blow coming until too late.

He had called out to Star, and saw her turn to look, when a whirling limb of the great tree rose from the water directly in front of him. He could not avoid the blow, but managed to turn his face partially away before the jagged tip struck him across the forehead.

Consciousness was fading fast as he slipped beneath the surface. There was a sense of letting go, a release from the necessity to fight any longer. The water was warm and welcome, and he wanted to relax.

Then there was only darkness.

18
» » »

André tried to open his eyes and found them gummy with clotted blood. He rubbed his face with his knuckles and discovered a tender area above his eyebrows.

"Lie still, Sky-Eyes," came the soft, yet urgent voice of Pale Star. "You are hurt."

He struggled to fuller consciousness, and memory came flooding back. The river, the accident! With great effort, and further careful rubbing, he managed to open his eyes. His vision wavered in and out of focus.

Pale Star was squatting on the other side of a small fire, watching him.

"The others?"

He hesitated to ask.

"Dead."

"I saw Woodchuck go under. Your husband, too?"

She nodded, her face tragic but tearless.

"I think so. I looked downstream but did not find them."

André tried to lift his head, but the effort produced

such severe throbbing in his temples that he lay back again. Cautiously, he looked around.

It was night, the darkness further muffled by fog and drizzle. He wondered for a moment about the fire, then realized that Pale Star was experienced and resourceful. This led to another thought.

"Our supplies?"

"Gone."

The seriousness of their plight suddenly came home to him. He raised on an elbow, and sank back again with a moan.

"Lie still, Sky-Eyes."

He lay looking upward. Overhead a blanket was stretched across a rough frame of sticks. It formed a sort of lean-to that reflected the warmth of the fire.

Star saw him looking at the blanket.

"I found it in the river when I was looking for the others. I will fix a better shelter tomorrow."

Another question struck him.

"Our weapons?"

"Gone, too. I have my throwing-ax."

André felt at his waist.

"I have a knife."

"Yes. I saw. But your little gun is lost."

It would be very difficult to obtain food. Even so, if they did avoid starvation, they were almost completely helpless against any potential enemies. He wondered what tribes might inhabit this area, and how dangerous they might be to strangers.

All this was too much for his injured head to handle. He drifted in and out of troubled sleep. Sometimes it seemed that the pain in his temples woke him. On other occasions, he heard the girl moving around, bringing more fuel for the fire.

Once, he was cold. He was lying on the ground, but Pale Star had tried to cushion his bed with small branches and grasses. It was still cold and damp, and he would turn to catch the reflected warmth of the fire on his slowly drying buckskins.

He had no idea as to the time at each awakening. It was still dark. The overcast prevented any sight of the stars. Sometimes it seemed that he had been cold and wet forever; in pain, injured, sleeping and waking fitfully.

When he roused enough to think rationally, their predicament seemed even more hopeless. Here they were, in the middle of the unexplored wilderness, without food, practically unarmed, with no shelter and far from any help. He regretted his part in bringing the others of the party to their doom. Somehow, the Southwest Water Passage to India seemed unimportant now. The search had cost two lives, and would probably cost two more, his own and that of Pale Star.

He looked across the fire and saw that she was not there. A flash of terror struck him at the thought that without her he was completely helpless. But no, she would not abandon him. Surely she had merely gone for more firewood.

He had not thanked her for her help. Now it occurred to him to wonder how he had escaped the river. He remembered slipping beneath the warm and welcoming water. The girl must have pulled him out. She had saved his life, and he had not even thanked her. He would be sure to do so the moment she returned.

Even with this resolve, he drifted off to sleep again. He woke, perhaps a moment later, perhaps after many hours. Pale Star was replenishing the fire again. That was good, he thought sleepily. He was becoming chilled again.

She looked over at him and saw that he was awake. She moved around the fire and knelt beside him.

"Are you resting better?"

He nodded weakly. Only then did he see that she was trembling with the night's chill. He touched her hand, and it was like ice. Her teeth were chattering.

"Sky-Eyes," she stated firmly, as if it required great resolve, "I am sorry, but we must share the shelter. We have no other warmth."

Remorse came flooding over him. Not only had he failed to thank her for saving his life and caring for him, he had also failed to notice that the girl was suffering from the chill of the night.

"Of course," he mumbled.

She crawled into the lean-to and snuggled beside him.

It was nothing but necessity, he told himself repeatedly, a matter of survival. The shared warmth of their bodies was pleasant and comfortable.

He was drifting off to sleep again when he felt some uneven object under his flank. He shifted position, then discovered that it was in the pocket of his own buckskin shirt. It was his oilskin-wrapped journal.

He wondered for a moment whether it was completely destroyed. It did not matter, he realized. His mission had failed. Completely depressed, he drifted off to sleep once more.

19

» » »

The day dawned gray and forbidding, as before. Pale Star rose and replenished the fire.

"You pulled me out of the river?" André asked.

"Yes."

The girl seemed slightly self-conscious about it.

"I wanted to thank you."

"It is nothing; I would do the same for anyone."

Rebuffed, he still continued.

"I am sorry about your husband. He was my friend."

"He was a good man. Woodchuck, also."

"Yes."

"I will mourn them today."

He was puzzled, and she saw his confusion.

"My people sing the Mourning Song. It honors the dead."

"I see."

"Later, I sing. Now, I go to find food."

She tucked the ax into the band around her waist and stepped away through the foggy timber. André wondered what she could possibly find to eat.

After a little while, he managed to sit up. He waited for the dizziness to subside, and moved gingerly to sit with his back against a tree for support. He could hear the murmur of the river to his left. Apparently the girl had carried or dragged him to higher ground some distance away, since he could not see the river from here. He marveled again at her stamina. He must do his best to recover quickly so that he would be no burden to her.

At this thought of the future, he remembered his journal, and fumbled it out of the pocket. Carefully he unwrapped the outer oilskin packet. There had been only a little leakage at one corner. Most of the manuscript would be intact, though water-marked.

He rewrapped and tied the packet. As soon as opportunity offered, he would dry the pages and further assess the damage. For now, he could not accomplish it in the fog and dampness. He returned the journal to its pocket. Again, he reminded himself, it did not matter much. The mission had failed. It was only out of the regimentation of his military background that he felt the need to document the fate of the expedition.

Toward midday, Star returned. She carried a rabbit, dangling in one hand, and a short, stout stick in the other. Over her shoulder was slung another trade blanket. She dropped her burdens.

"We eat, Sky-Eyes!"

Then her eyes dropped, and she indicated the blanket.

"I found the tree downstream. Part of one of the canoes. The blanket was caught in the branches."

"Any sign—?"

"No, Sky-Eyes. They are gone."

"You said you will mourn?"

"Yes. We survive, then we mourn. Let me use your knife?"

She pointed at the rabbit.

"I will skin the rabbit," he offered, "if you wish to sing for them."

Her face lightened.

"It is good. I will go to the river."

She handed him the rabbit and stepped down the slope. André was not used to such a chore, but believed he could handle the task. It did not seem difficult. After a false start or two, he had no trouble.

Down by the river, he could hear the plaintive wail of the Mourning Song rising and falling in pitch and volume. He wished that he could do or say something to help.

He did not know how long the Mourning Song might take, but he cut a green stick on which to cook the rabbit. He arranged others to prop over the fire and then spitted the skinned carcass and set it to cook.

He was pleased that this activity was not as devastating to him as it would have been earlier. The odor of cooking meat was good, and his spirits began to rise a little.

Star returned from the river at about the time the food was ready.

"I did not know how long the Mourning Song takes," he apologized.

"It is all right." She nodded. "It is best to mourn for three days, but sometimes it cannot be. I will sing a little while each morning."

"Is there a way I can mourn?"

Her face softened in a smile.

"I think not, Sky-Eyes. They will know that you mourn them."

They divided the rabbit between them and ate eagerly.

"Star, how did you catch the rabbit?"

"The throwing-stick." She pointed to the stick she had been carrying.

It was a little longer than his forearm, and as thick as his wrist, heavy and straight.

"Our children use it," she explained. "It is good for small game. I was considered expert with the sticks as a child."

"With good reason," André observed, waving a well-picked bone.

"Sky-Eyes, there is a spring near here. Can you walk there? I have nothing to carry water."

"I think so."

He had been on his feet only once since the accident, but he felt better with a little food. He pulled himself erect and stood swaying a little while he waited for the wave of dizziness to pass.

"Here, lean on me."

She put an arm around his waist and steadied him, leading him toward the slope. The dizziness lessened, and he began to feel better for the activity. On the way back, they gathered armfuls of damp firewood to dry out by the fire for later use. The exercise had caused some headache, but he was beginning to feel more confidence.

They returned to the makeshift camp site.

"Now," Star stated, "I will make a better shelter. Can you dry the blankets by the fire?"

"Of course."

He spread the damp blankets over branches of firewood, turning and warming to dry them. Star cut brush and roofed the slanting top of the lean-to to shed the drizzling rain that continued to fall intermittently.

By the time darkness fell, they were ready for a much more comfortable night.

20

» » »

May, the day not certain. Our mission has ended in failure. Brûle and Sergeant Cartier are dead, drowned when our canoes capsized. Pale Star and I have survived for the present.

We are camped by the junction of two rivers, recovering from our injuries. It seems unlikely that we can survive, as we have no food and no weapons, but I keep this journal in case someone may find it.

André lay awake in the lean-to, comfortable and warm in dry blankets. Cuddled next to him lay the sleeping girl. He was painfully aware of her presence, of the warm softness of her body.

Nothing had been said since the first night, when they had snuggled for the warmth that meant survival. Neither had mentioned the possibility of separate shelters, which would be rather impractical, or of separate blankets, which would not. They had continued to sleep together for the warmth and security that it provided.

Not that André had failed to consider more. He would

have loved to hold this girl as lovers do, but felt reluctant. He was still awed somewhat by her beauty. Theoretically, she was accessible now, but his strict religious upbringing held him in check. After all, he reminded himself, it had been only a few days since this woman's husband was killed.

As close as they had become by their joint efforts in survival, there was a point beyond which his ethics would not let him go. He could not insult the memory of his dead friend, the husband of the girl who had saved his life. He must avoid any advances or the appearance of any.

Therefore, he lay frustrated in the darkness, his back to the warm body next to him. It had been three days since the accident. He was feeling stronger daily. His head wound was healing well.

Star's throwing stick had kept them supplied, though thinly, with rabbits and squirrels. They had kept the skins to use for waterskins or for other purposes.

Meanwhile, they were working together to construct a bow and arrows. It would be crude but usable, and would enable them to obtain better food. They had already seen deer in the woods.

Nothing had been said about the future yet. Concentration had been on survival. Soon they must make some decisions, André knew. They had no canoe to go back, and no means to obtain one. They could not stay here indefinitely, though that thought did offer interesting fantasies. Equally impractical seemed the continuation of the mission or the search for Pale Star's people. They *must* talk about it.

Next to him in the darkness, there was a long, sobbing sigh.

"Star, you are awake?"

"Yes, Sky-Eyes. I grieve."

"I am sorry. I thought you were asleep."

He turned on his back. Perhaps now would be the time to talk.

"Sky-Eyes . . ." She spoke tentatively. "It was my fault."

"What was?"

"The accident."

"No, no, you must not blame yourself."

"But I knew we were passing the mouth of the other river. I tried to conceal it."

André was astonished.

"But how could you know? You have never been here before."

"Yes, I have. I lied."

"*Why*, in God's name?"

"I wanted to go home."

She was crying softly now.

"I wanted it so much that I caused my husband's death, and Woodchuck's."

André was still having a hard time understanding. Still, if the girl had this strong an urge to go home, it might answer the problem of plans for the future. Perhaps, even, he could continue his mission.

"Star, it was an accident. We knew it would be dangerous. I regret it too, but you cannot blame yourself."

"Thank you, Sky-Eyes."

"Look, when we are ready, let us go to find your people."

"Really?"

"Of course. I can continue my mission."

There was a moment of silence, a long pause unnoticed by André.

"It is good," Star announced.

There was happiness in her voice, but then she became serious again.

"Sky-Eyes," she said quietly, "why do you hate me?"

"*Hate* you? I could never hate you."

"But you avoid me. You have never spoken unless you must."

He was confused, embarrassed.

"Star, you must understand. You belonged to someone else. My friend, Brûle. I avoided you because I was afraid I was falling in love. I thought *you* disliked *me*."

Star chuckled, a beautiful liquid sound he had not heard for a long time.

"You, too?" she asked quietly.

"Of course. I thought—"

"Shh . . . come here."

He turned and kissed her, and she responded, warm and yielding and full of pent-up emotion.

"Oh, Star, I do love you," he murmured.

Sometime later, they both lay looking through the treetops at the stars. Many things had cleared this night, even the weather. They could begin to plan their journey.

But just now there seemed no hurry. She snuggled against his shoulder.

"Sky-Eyes," she whispered, "there is one more thing I should tell you."

"Yes," he answered sleepily, "what is it?"

"There is no Water Passage."

"What!"

He sat upright.

"That is right. There never was one."

"But you said—the river in your country—"

"No, you asked if it runs east and west. It runs *east.* All the rivers run east in my country. South and east."

"Then this Big River?"

"Runs south, straight to the Salty Big Water. Not west."

"The Gulf," he mused.

"I do not know. All the rivers this side of the mountains run into this one."

"The mountains? You know where they are?"

"Of course. To the west. One of our bands lives there."

"Star, this is important. You knew all this, but did not tell us?"

"No one asked me. And I wanted to go home. Do you hate me now, Sky-Eyes?"

André chuckled.

"How could I hate you?"

He lay back down and cuddled her to him.

"You have just given me a different mission!"

21
» » »

May; day unknown. I have been given new information that affects our mission. I have learned that the Big River we had been traveling runs straight south to the Gulf, not southwest to the Pacific. There are mountains to the far west of this prairie country, I am told.

I will progress westward overland to explore the country. It appears there is an abundance of game and fur, and fertile land. If, as it now appears, there is no Southwest Passage, it seems prudent at least to explore the possibility of settlement.

Pale Star, widow of the scout Brûle, will guide me.

When the sun rose, the two who had shared the passionate embrace were almost embarrassed by each other's presence. André was perhaps the most affected. He could not reconcile his actions with the recent death of his friend. In retrospect, he could not believe that he could have behaved in this way. Brûle had been dead only a matter of days, and he, André, had already become involved in an affair with the scout's widow.

No, not an affair, he tried to convince himself. It was more than that. How could anything that seemed so good and so right be wrong?

He watched the girl as they moved around the make-shift camp. She did not seem as concerned by their actions as he. At least, not as concerned as he felt. Well, he supposed, time would reveal her inner feelings. As for himself, he was more hopelessly in love than ever, despite twinges of conscience.

"We must make plans," he told her. "We go overland from here?"

The girl nodded.

"We could go up the other river, to the west, if we had a canoe. But the river is in flood anyway. Yes, we go overland."

André had no way of knowing that Star was not completely comfortable with river travel. It was fast and usually easy, but her background was that of the plains. The power of the deep swift water was a threat that always gnawed at the back of her mind. It had taken every bit of her courage to turn and dive beneath the surface to rescue the unconscious Sky-Eyes.

The guilt that she felt was of a slightly different type. She wondered, even now, if she might have been able to save her husband. She had seen the canoe strike and become impaled. She had watched the jagged limb as it knocked Sky-Eyes unconscious into the water. She had braved the current to save him. Yet, only a few strokes away, her husband was dying, pulled under by the treacherous river. Now she must live with this doubt. Could she have saved him? Was her preoccupation with Sky-Eyes actually responsible for her husband's death? It was not an easy thought. She would spend much time in the dead of the night, thinking, wondering.

As to the sharing of the blanket of Sky-Eyes, that bothered her very little. Hunting Hawk was dead, and life must go on. Hawk would understand, and life is for the living. Besides, now that she knew the true feeling of Sky-Eyes, it would be good to share his blanket.

He had seemed a little embarrassed this morning. She wondered if he, too, thought that he might have saved

Hawk. But no, he had had no chance. He must be concerned with loyalty to his friend. Yes, that would be it.
And she must show him that it would be right for them
to be together.

She smiled to herself and continued to make plans for
travel. Sky-Eyes sat scraping an arrow shaft to smooth it.
As soon as they had made a little more progress on the
arrows, they could start. Somewhere, they would manage
to kill a deer or a buffalo, and that would provide food for
the journey.

She did not know how far they must travel exactly,
but she would know when they arrived. They would
reach the country of the People at the River of Swans.
There they would search for the Eastern band, who could
tell them the whereabouts of the other bands. Then she
could rejoin her family, with the Southern, or Elk-dog,
band.

Beyond that, she did not plan. Much would depend on
Sky-Eyes, and how they were relating to each other by
that time. She entertained a vague hope that he would be
content to stay with her people, and not push west to the
mountains. But time would tell.

Star smiled to herself again at the memory of the
night, the comfortable warmth of blankets shared in love.
She walked over and placed her hand casually on his
shoulder as he worked.

"Is this right?" He smiled up at her, presenting a smooth
arrow shaft for her inspection.

"It is good, Sky-Eyes," she told him. "Now I will work
on feathers and points."

She knew that their best efforts would result in crude
arrows that might be laughed at by the weapons-makers
of the People. This, however, was a matter of survival.
Crude though they might be by a craftsman's standards,
their arrows could bring down large game. In fact, they
must.

They now required feathers, to make their arrows fly
true, and some sort of point. That would not be easy. A
keen, well-balanced stone point was practically out of
the question. They could, however, create a substitute.

She had carefully saved the bones from the rabbits

they had eaten. After breaking them in pieces, she had rubbed the fragments on a sandstone until they began to assume usable shapes. These would be sharpened and bound to the end of the arrow shaft. For that purpose, strips of rabbit and squirrel skin were already soaking in a muddy puddle to remove the fur and produce rawhide.

Star had been gathering feathers, too. Blue-gray wing quills from beneath the trees of a heron rookery a short distance away were saved for the purpose.

She stripped the feather from the quill and cut it to length, to tie to the arrow shaft with one of her slender strips of rawhide. She was just tying the knot, stretching the skin flat to dry and tighten, when she heard an exclamation of surprise from Sky-Eyes. She turned quickly.

Across the fire, on the other side of the little clearing, stood three warriors. Star reached for her ax, but the man who appeared to be their leader quickly held up his hand in the sign for peace.

"We are friends," he protested in sign-talk. "We came to find you."

"*Find* us?" Star asked suspiciously.

"Of course. The other man asked us to look for you."

"The *other* man?"

"Yes. Your companion. He thought you, also, might have drowned when the canoes went under."

"You found only one?"

"Yes, he held on to a log and floated downstream."

"But we were *four*."

"He said so." The warrior shrugged. "But we have found no other. Could he be above here?"

"No," answered Star. "The canoes broke up here. We searched, too, but found nothing."

André still sat, staring in numb disbelief.

Mon dieu, he whispered to himself. *Which one!*

22

» » »

The trail wound among the trees, roughly parallel to the stream, but following the route of least resistance. For centuries, both human and animal inhabitants of the region had followed this trail.

Now their guides led the way rapidly south. André began to tire. It had not been many days since his narrow escape from drowning. Finally the girl called to the leader and motioned him to come back.

"We must rest," she signed, pointing to her companion. "Sky-Eyes has not recovered from the river yet."

"Of course," nodded the warrior. "We stop here."

Everyone sank to a sitting or squatting position. Star looked at the men, still slightly uneasy over this turn of events. She had had some time to think as they traveled, and her thoughts troubled her. Assuming that these strangers were friendly, which they certainly seemed to be, there were still unanswered questions. She did not know their tribe or their customs. They seemed cooperative enough, but what would they expect in return? The travelers had lost everything in the wreck and had nothing to trade.

The foremost question, of course, which nagged at her constantly, was that of the other survivor. She knew that it bothered Sky-Eyes too, though he had said nothing.

They had assumed that Hunting Hawk was dead. She had acted accordingly, giving herself freely to Sky-Eyes. Now it appeared that Hawk, too, had survived the crash by clinging to driftwood. It was not likely that the less experienced Woodchuck would be the survivor, while Hawk perished.

This presented a problem of a different sort for Pale Star. Her guilt at not having tried to save her husband was now completely overshadowed by another feeling. She had been unfaithful to him. If he was dead, she could give herself as she saw fit, and she had done so, freely and without regret. Now, if Hawk was alive, her actions had been wrong. She knew that in some tribes this would be considered unimportant. Some men even freely lent their wives to others, sometimes for a price.

Her upbringing, however, did not allow for this laxity in behavior, and now her conscience was bothering her considerably. How would Hawk react? He had always respected her beliefs and customs, and now she herself had broken the marriage customs of her people.

With a great deal of dread, she thought of the long journey across the plains to her own country. A little while earlier, she had looked forward to it with anticipation. She could imagine the shared warmth of Sky-Eyes' blanket under the prairie stars.

One thing she could not imagine was how she could travel and sleep with Hawk while across the fire, cold and alone, slept Sky-Eyes. Could she choose between them? Would she be able to?

She owed so much to Hunting Hawk, who had saved her life. Their years together had been good. She had been a good wife to him. Only since the coming of Sky-Eyes had she become confused. Could she leave her husband for the outsider? She questioned it, but a few days ago she had been ready to leave him for the chance to return to her tribe.

That, of course, had been before she knew of Sky-Eyes' love for her. That knowledge had made many changes in her thoughts and feelings, but now caused even greater confusion.

What would the two men feel? She had had men fight over her before. Yes, even kill for possession of her. That had had great emotional impact. She still had night visions of the crazed Three Owls and his fight with his cousin.

In a way, this would be worse. Never before had there been a potential conflict between two men whom she respected and loved. *Aiee*, this would be difficult. She hoped they would not feel it necessary to fight over her. Still, she did not see how she could prevent it if they chose to do so. She must tread very cautiously and not do anything to bring anger to either man.

"How are you called?" one of the warriors signed, attempting to start a conversation.

"I am Pale Star. He is Sky-Eyes."

The other nodded.

"You come from far away?"

"Yes. We go to my people."

She pointed to the west.

"How far to your village?"

"Not far," he answered. "We will reach there before dark."

Then a thought occurred to her. This was the general area where her foster father had obtained a canoe, years before.

"Tell me," she gestured, "do you know a chief named Hunts-in-the-Rain?"

The warrior's eyes widened perceptibly.

"Of course! His village is only one sleep below ours. How do you know him?"

"He is a friend of my father."

Star felt considerably better. Somehow, the mere knowledge that there was someone in the region who knew her was a comfort to her. It gave her a sense of security.

The leader now rose.

"Come. We go now."

They struck the trail again.

With frequent rest stops, it was late in the day before they began to see signs of a settlement ahead. A canoe on the river, a branch of the trail leading aside to a muddy river landing.

Sun Boy's torch was casting long shadows when Star smelled the smoke of the village ahead. She smiled at the thought she had just had. Sun Boy. It had been many seasons since she had thought of the setting sun as the legendary Sun Boy of her people. It must be that at last she was really convinced she was going home.

For a moment, she almost felt good. Then the knotty problem of her relationship with Sky-Eyes came back to depress her spirit again. She studied his back as he walked ahead of her on the trail. Once more, she admired the span of his shoulders, the proud swing of his body as he walked. Even though she knew he was near exhaustion, he still carried himself with pride.

Now they could see the lodges of the village ahead, built of poles and thatched with grass on the top. She had found these dwellings oppressively close and smelly on her previous contact, but now the familiar shapes seemed welcome.

Someone shouted, and people began to gather to watch them arrive. Soon she would know for certain about Hunting Hawk.

"Where is our companion?" she asked one of the warriors in sign-talk.

"He went with the canoes to look for you," the man answered.

He shouted a question to a youth standing nearby and then turned back to her with the answer.

"They have not returned yet. Come, we will eat, and they should be back soon."

Star's heart was heavy. She must still wait, and it was not an easy task.

23
» » »

André was nearly stumbling with fatigue as they neared the village. He managed to keep up appearances, walking tall and remembering to assume a military bearing.

He happened to see the question asked by Pale Star, and the answer. The other survivor was absent, gone on a search mission by canoe. *Mon dieu*, the suspense was painful. His emotions had been yanked up and down so much in the past few days. It was becoming extremely frustrating.

At first, it had seemed that he must completely avoid the girl who had so changed his life. It would jeopardize his mission to become involved. Then, without his knowing quite when and how, the reasons changed. He kept apart from her out of respect for her husband, who had become his friend. At the same time, he had come to admire and respect her all the more. Still, she was untouchable.

Suddenly and without warning, her husband was lost, and he and Pale Star were thrown together. They had shared physical warmth, first for survival, then for love.

With Brûle dead, there was no reason to stay apart. Even in the aftermath of tragedy, the future seemed bright.

André was just beginning to revel in the ecstasy of an ideal relationship with this, the finest of all women, when disaster struck again. He hated to think of it in that way, but he could not help it. It had seemed so right, the way things were working out. There was nothing to keep them apart.

The news that there had been another survivor came with a jarring conflict of emotions. His first thought was to wish that it was Cartier. Then immediately he felt guilt for wishing the death of his friend Brûle. Even more powerful was the guilt that stemmed from his having betrayed the friendship.

Now he could hardly bear the thought of the continued journey. He imagined the cool starry nights with the girl sharing another's blanket, and the thought was intolerable. Yet, they must go on or go back, and either way the three would be thrown together. How cruel fate could be!

Star had hardly looked at him since the three warriors had arrived at their camp. He was certain that her feelings were much like his. Confused, guilty, anxious.

They were entering the village now, and she spoke to him in French.

"It is the proper thing to visit the chief. They will take us there. You should talk to him, in signs. I will help you."

André nodded. He knew that much would depend on the dignity with which this meeting was conducted.

They were ushered into a dim lodge that smelled of smoke and fish and human bodies. The travelers and their guides moved forward to where an elderly man sat on a spread robe.

"This will be the chief," Star said softly in French. "Tell him we are honored to be guests in his village."

Slowly and with help from the girl, André made the signs.

"It is good," replied the chief. "Your accident was a bad thing."

"Yes," acknowledged André, "and we have lost one of our party."

The chief nodded.

"The other will return soon. Sit, we will eat."

André found that he had little appetite, but attempted to eat enough of the smoked fish to appear appreciative. The chief made light conversation in sign-talk, asking about the weather and their journey.

It was extremely frustrating for the young man. How could he possibly sit and eat and make small talk about the weather when such important things were brewing? At any moment, the search party would return. Depending on who lived, this could be the most momentous event of André's life.

He watched Pale Star maintain her composure. It was certain that she was under similar pressure, but she seemed perfectly under control; calm and relaxed. It bothered André considerably that the chief seemed quite attracted to her. The man kept staring at her as they ate and talked. Finally, irritated, André spoke to her in French.

"Why does he keep staring?"

"I do not know, Sky-Eyes. He finds me pleasant to look upon, maybe."

"But there is more, no?"

"I think so. We will watch."

This conversation was carried on as a quiet aside, between scraps of sign-talk.

"It is customary to bring gifts to a chief whose village we visit. Maybe you should regret that we have none," the girl suggested.

André asked a sign or two, and Star made suggestions. Then he began.

"My chief, we carried gifts, but they were lost in the river. I am sorry we cannot honor you properly."

"It is nothing." The other dismissed the apology with the wave of a hand.

Somehow this denial did not seem final. André felt that something was being left unsaid. Then, at his elbow, Star suddenly seemed to understand.

"*Aiee!*" she said softly.

"What is it?"

"I think I know."

"Tell me, Star."

"We have nothing to give him. He may ask for me."

André felt the rage rise in him.

"No, no, Sky-Eyes. That is their way," she cautioned.

"But—"

"Be careful. If he asks, you must tell him I am your guide, and you cannot travel without me."

"You mean he would—"

"Maybe not, but he keeps looking at me. You should be prepared if he does ask."

André fought down anger and jealousy and attempted to appear calm. Star ate, smiled, and continued to act as comfortable as a guest should. He did not see how the girl could remain so calm.

Finally the chief appeared to finish his meal. He belched loudly, motioned a woman to remove the woven tray on which his food had been brought. Then he turned to André.

"Now," he began, "let us talk of your woman here."

André clenched his teeth tightly. This was becoming a very dangerous situation. He was well aware of Star's whispered warning to be careful.

The chief leaned forward toward the girl with a look of absorbed interest. Slowly, he extended a hand toward her slim waist. André was ready to leap to her defense, to fight for both their lives. The pointing finger wavered and stopped.

"This ax," the old man signed, "why does a woman carry an ax? I have never seen such a weapon."

André almost laughed aloud in relief. It was not the girl's body that the chief had been ogling, but the ax at her waist. It was the weapon that he coveted.

Quickly, Star whispered to him in French.

"Their women do not carry weapons. Offer him the ax for supplies and help."

André could now see how the scene was unfolding. He extended his open palm toward Star, and she placed the ax in his hand.

"My chief," André signed, "this ax has strong medicine. It is yours."

He handed the ax to the other man, who now beamed broadly as he examined it. Firelight reflected from its keenly honed edge. The chief tested it with a thumb and uttered a pleased exclamation.

"They have few iron weapons," Star was explaining. "This is a very great gift."

André nodded. This was going well, now that they understood the game.

"Should I ask about supplies now?"

"No, he will know that. We wait."

A commotion was heard outside, and someone stuck a head through the doorway to speak to the chief. He turned to the visitors.

"Your companion has returned," he signed.

Both André and Star turned quickly to look at the doorway. A man in buckskins was stooping to enter the lodge. He straightened, and the firelight shone on his face as he turned a broad smile to the others.

It was Cartier.

"Woodchuck!" gasped Star.

She turned to look at André, her eyes speaking untold volumes. He met her meaningful glance for a moment and then scrambled to his feet to greet the sergeant. They embraced briefly, tears of joy spilling down Cartier's face.

"I thought you were all drowned," he muttered. "Brûle?"

"Gone," said André simply.

"I thought so."

He turned to the girl.

"I am sorry, madame."

Star shrugged.

"Things happen. The river has claimed him and spared us. I have mourned him."

Sergeant Cartier appeared a trifle confused. There was a finality here that he had not expected. He looked from the girl to André and back again.

"You two?"

André nodded, embarrassed somehow at the implication.

"Sergeant, we must talk."

"It is good, Lieutenant. I could see your feelings before. It is good for you to have each other."

André felt the need for fuller explanation, but Cartier left no opportunity. If the man had been somewhat critical, even, it would have been easier. As it was, the guilt feelings rose again to plague André. Frustrated, he did not answer.

"We go on?" Cartier was asking.

"Yes. But we must talk about that, too. About our mission."

A woman entered the lodge and held one of the woven rush mats before Cartier.

"Eat, now," motioned the old chief.

Cartier seated himself and began.

"Later," said André, "later we will talk. There is much to tell."

24

》 》 》

May, late in the month. Possibly even early June. We have lost count of civilization's calendar. This is called by the natives the Moon of Roses.

We have found Sergeant Cartier, alive. The three of us are traveling overland toward the country of Pale Star's people. This is a vast open plain, a grassland that could be made to raise crops. There is still an abundance of game and of furbearing animals.

We have seen great herds of the hump-backed cattle called bison or buffalo. They are found quite palatable, and some tribes appear to subsist largely on this native beef. I believe domestic cattle would do well here likewise.

We are traveling almost due west, guided by the woman Pale Star.

The three travelers sat around the fire and listened to the night sounds. Nearby a night-bird called, repeating a melodious phrase. *Pour Pierre?* André imagined that the creature said, over and over.

From a thicket of scrubby timber a little distance away came the occasional call of an owl.

"That is *kookooskoos*," observed Star. "The hunting owl."

"Yes, we have them in our country," André answered. "Their call is a little different."

They were quiet again for a time, and a cricket chirped happily from somewhere in the grass. From a distant ridge a coyote called to its mate, and the other answered.

"The sky is so big," spoke Cartier, a little in awe.

"Yes, Woodchuck," answered Star. "When I was stolen and carried away, this was what I missed most of all."

"How old were you, Star?" asked André.

"Fourteen, maybe fifteen summers. I will tell you about it sometime. Not now. I need to stretch my eyes."

She leaned back against his shoulder, luxuriating in the expanse of prairie and sky. She was delighted that André shared her feeling. It was obvious in the way he gazed into the distant sunset or watched the skies at night. Some outsiders, she knew, never developed a feel for the spirit of the plains. Others found it immediately. She was pleased that Sky-Eyes felt it.

Woodchuck, too, she could tell, had quickly become a lover of the open country. Sky-Eyes had explained to him the changed nature of the mission, and Woodchuck had elected to go on.

It was not merely military duty. Sky-Eyes had told him about the Elk-dog People and the mountains far to the west. He had suggested that if the sergeant wished, he could carry a report of the mission back to the fort.

Or they could move on to the west and report back together when their modified mission was finished. Woodchuck had taken little time to choose the latter alternative.

The thought of returning to Mishi-ghan worried the girl a little. But that was a long way off. For now, she was going home. Home, in the company of the man she now regarded as husband. She knew that once among her people, she would not wish to leave. She would rather imagine Sky-Eyes adapting to her ways. Already, his growing love for the big skies and far horizons of her home seemed to promise more.

However, the girl was able to take each day as it came. This ability to adapt had brought her through difficult times before, and would do so again.

"How far do you think we must travel now, Star?" Sky-Eyes asked.

"I do not know exactly. I have never come this way before."

He smiled.

"Really?"

This was a small joke between them. He was teasing her for her previous deception.

"Yes, really, Sky-Eyes. It is a few sleeps yet. I will know when we reach the River of Swans. I will tell you."

She snuggled against him, enjoying the warmth of his body against the night chill.

"And your people will be in that area?"

"Maybe not. That is the edge of their country. They move around."

Sky-Eyes had not quite been able to understand that custom, even though they had encountered a small band on the move during their river journey. They had watched the moving nomads with their horses, baggage, women, children, and dogs as they straggled along across the hill. The lieutenant had watched with some degree of wonder and fascination. Now he was curious again.

"How will we find them?"

"Ask someone. The Growers."

"You have mentioned the Growers before. Who are they?"

"They stay in one place. They raise corn and pumpkins and beans. Other tribes trade skins and meat for these things."

"But how will they know?"

"They trade with all tribes, and they will know everyone's camping place this summer."

"And your people will be somewhere near?"

"They might be. Well, not my own people, but one of the bands of our tribe. Our Eastern band camps from the River of Swans to the area south of our Big River, usually. But if we find them, they will know where the Elk-dog band, and my own family, will be."

"How many bands are there?"

"Five, now. There was once a sixth, but they were lost in long-ago times."

"You must tell me more about your people. Could I learn to speak your tongue?"

Star was greatly pleased.

"Of course. I will teach you. But until you learn, you can use sign-talk."

It is good, she smiled to herself. There had been a time when she had despaired of ever returning to her people. Now things seemed to be going better. She snuggled closer to Sky-Eyes, and he drew the warm blanket around her shoulders.

It was good.

25
>> >> >>

*T*he Moon of Roses. Last night we arrived at the river which is called by the natives the River of Swans. There are nesting waterfowl, and the area is charming. This stream is not large, but is pleasing in its beauty. A broad grassy flood plain seems to have good potential for crops.

We have stopped for information at a village which Pale Star refers to as Growers. These are farmers, who trade their produce to surrounding tribes of hunters.

Our supplies, which we obtained at a river village after the accident, are holding up well, with what game we kill. These natives seem to have had no contact with whites. We traded one ax for the supplies we needed. None had seen weapons of iron or steel before.

We will push on westward in search of Pale Star's tribe, who are apparently nomads.

They reached the river just before sunset, when the shadows were beginning to creep across the valleys of the prairie. The three stood on the crest of a low ridge and looked to the west.

106

The stream meandered across a lush grassy plain, becoming smaller in the distance, until, gilded by the setting sun, it appeared to blend with the sky in a blaze of glory. Waterfowl dotted the orange of the sky, and a lone heron beat his way slowly toward some distant rookery.

"Marvelous!" André spoke softly. "Is this your Big River?"

"No, Sky-Eyes. It is to the north, maybe two, three sleeps. It is bigger. This is the River of Swans."

"It is a beautiful place."

"Yes," Star agreed simply. "Here begins the country of my people."

"Which side of the river?"

"Both. There is no boundary, such as your people have, Sky-Eyes. The river runs from the northwest, through the home of the People. Our Northern band usually camps north of the river."

"You have spoken of other bands. Yours is the Southern band?"

"Yes. But the nearest is probably the Eastern band. We will ask for them."

"Ask the Growers, no?"

"Yes."

"And how do we find the Growers?"

The girl extended a pointing arm to the northwest and the setting sun. Golden rays seemed to bathe her face and hair, and the excitement in her eyes emphasized the radiance.

"We follow the river. Somewhere along the river there will be a town."

"How far?"

"I do not know. It does not matter. We go in the right direction."

They had traveled rapidly after leaving the river village. The weather had favored them. Only once they paused for a day and sought shelter in heavy timber while a noisy storm crashed and boomed.

On one other occasion, the three hid for part of an afternoon while a well-armed party of horsemen wandered casually across the open landscape.

"They are probably hunters, and would do us no harm," whispered Star. "But I do not know them. We wait."

Now, in her own territory, the girl was a changed person. Confident, eager, ready to push on. It was two more days before they found signs of the Growers. It was early morning, and Star paused on the highest point in the immediate area to survey the country to the west.

With the sun at their back, details not seen the evening before became clearer. The river's course, the scattered groves along the banks, and the broad flats of the flood plain all became clear. Grassy low hills lay to the north, giving promise of new sights and sounds beyond. There were scattered bands of buffalo and elk in the far distance.

"There!" suddenly said the girl, pointing.

"Where? What is it?"

"The village."

"I do not see it."

"Look, Sky-Eyes. You have not learned to see the prairie yet."

André searched the landscape as keenly as he could and still saw nothing. The course of the river was marked by the thin line of trees they had noted before. Now, in addition, there was a cottony mist of fog drifting along the surface or hanging heavily among the willows.

"Look just beyond the bend"—Star pointed—"where the river turns to the south for a little. See the smoke?"

In the distance, following her pointing finger, the others could distinguish the river's bend. Just to the left, it was possible to imagine that the fog lay a little heavier.

"Smoke lies differently than fog," observed the girl. "It is of different color, too."

Now that it had been called to his attention, André could plainly see the differences. The smoke was of a slightly bluish hue against the misty white of the morning's fog. And there was indeed a difference in its behavior. Fog lay lazily in patches and layers, while the smoke rose vertically and then spread in a soft blanket over the river.

"They are different spirits," Star explained.

That was as good an explanation as any, it seemed.

They started down the hill. Even at a steady pace, it was nearly midday before they approached the village.

"How do we know they are friendly?" André wondered.

"Growers are friends to all," Star explained. "They must trade with others. They cannot take sides in the quarrels of others, because their crops could be destroyed."

"I see. They could be easily hurt."

"Yes. That is why they must stay—what is the word?"

"Neutral?"

"Yes. On neither side."

"But we do not come to trade."

"Yes, but we might sometime."

"Do you speak their tongue?"

"Only a little, and it is a long time ago. We will use sign-talk."

They were now among cultivated patches of corn and pumpkins. André looked curiously at the unfamiliar crops.

Then they found themselves entering a winding path among half-buried dwellings. Children stared and dogs barked. A man rose from a seated position beside one of the lodges and came toward them, right hand raised in greeting. The three travelers stopped.

"Greetings, my chief," Star signed. "I am Pale Star, of the Elk-dog People. Can you tell me where they are camped this season?"

"Of course." The man nodded eagerly. "They have been here. They left only three sleeps ago."

He pointed to the broad meadow across the river. There they could see the close-cropped grass, the circles on the sod where lodges had stood. Here and there lay a broken or discarded lodgepole, a worn-out moccasin, or a clean-picked bone of buffalo. There was nothing more.

The People had departed.

26
>> >> >>

André's heart sank.

"Now what? They are gone!"

"No, this is good, Sky-Eyes. Now we know where they are. If they have gone only three days, we can find them easily."

She turned back toward the Grower.

"This was the Eastern band of the People? The band of Chief Small Ears?"

"No, no. Small Ears is dead, for three winters. The band is led by Red Feather."

"This is the band we seek," Star said in an aside to André. "They have a new chief. Small Ears was very old, even before I was taken away."

She turned back to sign-talk.

"Did my people tell you where they were going?"

"To your Sun Dance."

"Where is it this year?"

"Cedar River, maybe."

"It does not matter, my chief. We will follow their trail."

The trail of the moving band was broad and plain. A blind person could have followed it. They could see its meandering course as far into the distance as the farthest ridge of hills.

"They are moving the whole village," Star explained to her two companions. "They use their lodgepoles to carry all their possessions on pole-drags."

She pointed to the myriad of deeply scored marks in the sod, all running parallel, toward the horizon.

"All we have to do is follow this trail until we catch up to them."

"But, Star," protested André, "they have a three-day start."

"That is true, Sky-Eyes. But they have the children and old persons. They will move slowly. It would be better if we had horses, but there are none to be had. We can catch them on foot."

They pushed ahead the same day, covering much distance before dark.

"We will sleep a little," Star announced. "There is no need for a watch here. Then we rise with the moon to travel."

Sometime before dawn, they found the first camp of the People. The ashes of cooking fires were cold, and the leaves on the temporary brush shelters were dry and withered.

"But now," explained Star, "we are only two sleeps behind them."

Even so, it was four more days before the trail seemed fresh. They found ashes still warm from last night's fires, and the horse droppings were moist enough to attract clouds of tiny gnats. Star picked up a worn-out moccasin, cast aside before leaving camp. She turned it slowly, playing with the thong that dangled a full hand's span from its attachment at the heel.

"It is the mark of my people," she spoke softly. "This heel-cord tells any stranger that these are the Elk-dog People."

"Like the uniform of a soldier?"

"Yes, maybe. They use it because it is good to show they are of the People."

"It is a thing of pride then."

"Yes, that is it. It is good to be a proud people."

She drew herself to her full height, chin up and shoulders squared. André was once more impressed by her queenly demeanor. Yes, he thought, it is good to take pride in heritage.

He could see the change in the girl, the sense of confidence, the excitement, from one day to the next. She had always seemed proud and confident, but there was a difference. Now she radiated, somehow, a sense of belonging. This was her land, the source of her being and of her strength. André thought of the simile of a queen returning to claim her kingdom after exile.

"We will overtake them tomorrow," predicted Star, tossing the worn moccasin aside.

She started on, with the others close behind, matching her long swinging stride.

It was late afternoon of the following day when the girl paused at the crest of a low ridge and pointed ahead. In the dim colorless confusion of distance, a sense of motion could be seen.

"They are preparing to stop for the night," Star observed.

André started to ask how she could tell, but thought better of it. He would try to reason it out.

A wisp or two of smoke rose straight upward against a dark slash of timber in the distance. Fires meant that they were pausing long enough to cook. In late afternoon, that meant a stop for the night. He was pleased by his abillty to reason this thing.

In the silence of the wind-swept prairie, he could now hear a faint buzz of noise and motion from the distant camp. It was like the dimly sensed, moving life-activity in a beehive. This, he knew, would be a mixture of shouts, conversation, barking dogs, and calling horses, as the big column drew itself together and consolidated for the night.

"Come," said Star, "we will just reach them by dark."

Twilight was falling as the three moved near the camp fires. There were curious looks, and yapping dogs ran out to meet them. Star paused beside the first of the fires and spoke to the woman who knelt there.

"Where is your chief's camp?"

The woman turned and pointed.

"Over there."

"Thank you, Mother."

André watched and listened with interest. He could understand very little of the People's tongue as yet, but such an exchange was easy to follow. He found that he understood a word or two, from Star's instruction as they had traveled.

People were looking at the newcomers curiously, at the unfamiliar style of their buckskins and equipment.

Star led the way among the fires, pausing once more to ask directions. She stopped before a family camp site where a dignified man was just feeding a couple of sticks to the evening fire.

"Red Feather?"

The chief straightened and turned.

"Yes?"

"Greetings, my chief. I am Pale Star, of the Elk-dog band."

He stared for a moment, as if trying to recall.

"Pale Star?"

"Yes, my chief. I was stolen five summers ago."

A broad smile split the chief's face.

"Of course, my child! I remember now. Your uncle is my friend Looks Far."

"Yes. This is my husband, Sky-Eyes, and our friend Woodchuck."

Red Feather nodded a greeting to the others.

"Come, sit. Share our meat."

"It is good, my chief. You are traveling to the Sun Dance?"

"Yes. It will be at Cedar River. You will travel with us?"

"If we may."

"Of course. You will be guests of my lodge. You must tell us of all that has happened."

It might be many sleeps before they reached Cedar River, but a great feeling of relief crept over Star's being that evening as they settled for the night.

At last, she was back among her own people. She was home.

27

» » »

The Moon of Roses. We have joined the Eastern band of Pale Star's Elk-dog People, and are traveling with them. They are tall, well formed, and handsome. They are experienced horsemen, and the quality of their mounts is excellent.

We are well accepted, in part due to the great help of Pale Star.

Our direction of travel is southwest. We are to meet the other bands of the tribe for an annual council, which is their custom. The land is fair, and fur, game, and fowl plentiful. It would be very desirable for expansion.

Sergeant Cartier sat with his back against a tree, whittling a dead stick he had picked up. As usual, he was surrounded by a group of children. There was something about the man that seemed to attract children. André had noticed it during their contacts with other tribes.

His smile, his easygoing manner, the gentleness of the man—all this was accepted instinctively by those who met him. When he was introduced to someone, it was not uncommon for the name Woodchuck to elicit a smile. It was appropriate, descriptive, and told much about him.

He had almost immediately attracted a following of children. Even with the language barrier, he seemed to have no problem with communication. Part of the attraction was his ability to whittle and carve interesting objects out of scraps of wood. Woodchuck was skillful with his belt knife and constantly created little animals and birds and willow whistles that he handed out to the children.

At first it seemed that there might be a problem. Some of the parents objected, afraid of possible harm from the "medicine" of the outsider. It took André and Cartier a little while to realize that these people had never seen steel knives before, and regarded the "medicine-knives" with awe.

Star laughed when they inquired about it, and told of her own reactions to the first steel knife she had seen.

It helped, of course, that the newcomers were guests in the lodge of the band chief, Red Feather. This, and the fact that Sky-Eyes was the husband of a woman of the People, lent an air of respectability.

So they traveled each day, riding borrowed horses. When Woodchuck dismounted, he was surrounded by his young admirers. He was always joking and laughing with them and creating toys. He had no idea that some of these simple creations, imbued with the medicine of the knife, would remain important to the recipients. Many a warrior of the People, in future seasons, would take pride that his medicine bag contained an object made by the medicine-knife of Woodchuck.

Among his young followers, or nearby, there always seemed to be an older girl. Woodchuck noticed her immediately because of her beauty. Her name, he learned, was Pink Cloud, and she was a daughter of their host Red Feather. The girl was easily of marriageable age, it appeared, but had not yet chosen a husband.

"It is a kind thing you do for them, Woodchuck," she said one day, using signs as well as words.

He was confused and embarrassed for a moment, but recovered quickly.

"It is nothing. It makes them happy," he signed.

"Yes. Children are important to my people. One who helps them is held in high regard."

The sergeant nodded self-consciously.

"I come from a big family. Seven brothers and sisters."

"*Aiee!* You have much to do with children!"

Both laughed, and that began their romance. They were seldom apart. Soon Pink Cloud was saving oddly shaped sticks for him to use in his carving, and sharing the delight of the children in the results.

The entire band viewed the blossoming romance with tolerant amusement, because both these young people were popular and well liked. It seemed a likely alliance.

Finally, a few days before they expected to meet the rest of the tribe, Cartier hesitantly approached André.

"Lieutenant, do you know the marriage customs of the People?"

"No"—André smiled—"but we can ask Star. You and Pink Cloud?"

The other nodded self-consciously.

"I have never wanted to marry anyone before."

"I know the feeling, my friend."

Star did not seem surprised.

"Of course, Woodchuck. Our custom is this: You ask her father's permission, and offer him something of value."

"But I have nothing of value."

"Then use your skill. Make something. A medicine-stick. I will help you."

Pink Cloud assisted also. The women chose the materials and colors, and Woodchuck began to carve. They were careful to conceal the activity from Chief Red Feather.

The stick chosen was of special shape, with an enlarged knob on one end and a hooked projection. Under the skilled knife of Woodchuck it quickly took shape.

"*Aiee!* An eagle's head!" exclaimed Pink Cloud.

The color of the wood was light, nearly enough white to give the impression of the eagle's head. Star saw what was needed and procured pigments for the eye and the yellow beak. She nodded in approval.

"Now the main part of the stick should be red and

yellow. These are sacred colors. You will need an eagle
feather, and maybe some fur to finish it. Yes, strips of
otter would be nice."

"But, Star, I have no otter skins or eagle feathers."

"Let me see what I can do, Woodchuck."

Apparently the friends of Pink Cloud proved helpful
and cooperative. At least, within another day, Woodchuck had all the needed materials. Pale Star made suggestions as to appropriate design and construction, and
supervised the effort.

Nearly everyone in the band knew what was happening except Red Feather. At least, he pretended not to
know. It might have been noted that the chief did not
seem unduly surprised when Woodchuck came to ask for
his daughter.

He did seem startled and pleased, however, by the
presentation of the beautiful eagle-headed medicine-stick.

"It is good," he nodded. "We will have the marriage at
the Big Council."

"But, Father," pleaded Pink Cloud, "there is much going
on at the Big Council. Much visiting, dancing, the Sun
Dance. Can we not marry sooner?"

Red Feather smiled tolerantly.

"*Aiee*, why not? I would probably be too busy at the
Council anyway!"

28
» » »

The marriage ceremony was held very simply at one of the night camps on the trail. Pale Star helped enthusiastically with the planning.

Red Feather seemed pleased and proud, ready to welcome a son to his lodge. His attitude toward the medicine-stick showed that he held it almost in reverence.

Star had also approached André with a strange request.

"Sky-Eyes," she began hesitantly, "you know that among my people marriage is not taken lightly."

"Yes, of course."

"And you know that we are one already."

"Yes."

"Well, then, could we—could it be—" She paused in frustration, took a deep breath, and continued, "Could we have a marriage ceremony, too?"

"Of course!"

He gathered her in his arms for a moment, then held her at arm's length.

"How do we do this?"

"It is simple. The girl's father spreads a robe over the

shoulders of the new couple. Red Feather can spread the robe, since my father is not here."

"That is all?"

"He says some words. It is a prayer—that we shelter and protect each other, and that our lodge shall be safe and happy."

"It is good."

Pale Star had been concerned over this more than she had been willing to admit. Her previous alliances had been either forced, against her will, or in a situation where she had little choice. Now, for the first time, here was a romance of her choosing, with no coercion or debt to repay.

She had reveled in the ecstasy that she shared with Sky-Eyes, but as she neared her own people, her own family, she became uneasy. She was, by any standards, the wife of the tall lieutenant, body and soul. She had never been more certain of anything. But there had never been a ceremony. Star had hesitated to mention it. Would Sky-Eyes misunderstand? Would he think she was demanding more than he wanted to give?

There was no real doubt in her mind that he was as dedicated to this union as she. It was only that she did not wish to force him to make any public statement that he was unsure of.

Her own concern was that when she approached her parents after the five-year absence, she could say, proudly and truthfully, "This is my husband." Star was pleased that he seemed to understand, that he agreed readily. She did not know the customs of his people, but she was aware that many of the soldiers were quite promiscuous, bedding with almost any woman. Somehow she felt that with Sky-Eyes, it was different.

For one thing, it was known that at the fort he had not frequented the lodges and tents of the camp followers. For another, he showed her gentleness and respect.

All in all, she was very pleased with his reaction to her suggestion.

"Of course."

There seemed little doubt in his mind that this was the proper course of action. How could it be, she wondered with a private little smile, that this outsider seemed to understand so easily her country and her people? Already he was making great progress in speaking her language.

The two couples were united in the ceremony of the robes at a night camp somewhere southwest of the River of Swans. The place had been chosen for its spring; a clear, cold stream that gushed out of a rocky hole under the hill.

The stars sparkled like the night fires of a thousand camps, and a soft south wind caressed the skin and stirred the leaves of the cottonwoods along the creek.

Red Feather stepped forward, carrying two buffalo robes. The four young people knelt, and the chief spread a robe around the shoulders of each couple. Then he raised his hands to the sky and intoned the prayer.

André, shoulder to shoulder with Star, felt her warmth. Her right thigh pressed against his left, and a lump rose in his throat. He wondered a little what his parents would think of this pagan rite, but it did not seem important.

Tonight he had participated in a ceremony that obviously had a deep religious significance for Pale Star and her people. It did not seem to matter that it was not a religion that was familiar to his world. His rather narrow world, he was beginning to think. He could see the depth of emotion, the sincerity, the meaning in the faces of friends and relatives around the fire.

He looked at the face of the girl, and she smiled at him. She had never looked more beautiful.

"Thank you, my husband," she whispered in French.

"For what?"

"For this. For letting us be married in the custom of my people."

"But you are of the People, and now, so am I."

He wondered, even as he said it, why he would make such a statement. It was true, he had come to admire and respect much about these people and their customs, their love of the big sky and the prairie. At times he could feel its spirit, and could understand the attraction that had led Star halfway across the continent to return to the land that had given her life.

He was confused by these feelings. There were times when he thought of himself as a soldier on an assignment, and that all other considerations were secondary. Then he would look at the vastness of the prairie sunset or the immense expanse of the night sky. He would listen to the song of the prairie stream or to the coyote's plaintive call to his mate on the other hill.

At these times, he would feel that primarily he was a man, a human being with a spirit that was part of this magnificent creation. A man who had been united in marriage by a simple ceremony to a daughter of this creation.

He was comfortable in this role. Comfortable. Yes, that was it. When he thought of these things, all seemed as it should be.

Especially right and fitting was his relationship to the girl who had intrigued, stimulated, fascinated him, and who now had become his wife.

Because now, no matter what else was right, wrong, disturbing, or puzzling in all of creation, Pale Star was his wife, and he her husband. And that, he reflected, was right.

29
>> >> >>

The Moon of Roses. We have now joined the major portion of the tribe who are called the Elk-dog People. Among themselves, they simply say "the People."

This is an amazing spectacle, hundreds of their conical skin tents or lodges scattered as far as the eye can see. The occasion is called the Sun Dance, where the scattered bands, some five or six, come together for this ritual each year. There are other ceremonies and dances and a major council, the Big Council.

We have also seen exhibitions of the expertise of these horsemen. It is my opinion that as light cavalry they rival any in Europe. Their feats of skill and daring are almost beyond description.

The first contact came one morning when a lone rider appeared on a ridge ahead. He stood watching for a moment, then wheeled his horse and disappeared.

"He goes to announce our coming," explained Pale Star.

It was nearly midday before they topped a low rise to

see horsemen approaching. The front of the column moved into the open and paused, allowing the rest of the band to join them for the meeting. Red Feather assumed a place of prominence in front of his band, flanked by a handful of subchiefs.

"What is going on?" André whispered.

"The chiefs prepare to meet the others," Star answered. "Now watch."

The approaching riders, some twenty in number, paused at a little distance, grouped themselves, and, at some signal from a leader, suddenly broke forward in a spectacular charge. André, even knowing this was a friendly meeting, felt the hair rise on his neck. The full-throated war cry that echoed across the prairie was a chilling thing. Horses fretted and danced nervously as the charging platoon thundered toward them, then veered at the last moment, to circle the band of Red Feather at a hard gallop.

A few young warriors, unable to sit still in the excitement of the moment, struck heels to their horses to join the newcomers. The war cry now rose from new throats. André glanced aside at Pale Star. She sat on her horse, eyes ablaze, entranced by the unfolding excitement.

"Come on!" she suddenly shouted.

She kicked her horse forward. André's mount, already excited, bolted to follow. Before he knew what was happening, André found himself riding with the circling warriors. It was intoxicating, the war cries, the pounding of a hundred hooves, the dust, and the pure joy of sharing the occasion.

He did not understand it all. In retrospect, it seemed impossible that he could have been so carried away by the excitement of this primitive demonstration. Centuries of civilization had peeled away in an instant, and he was one with the other sons of the prairie.

Just now, they swept into the current of exuberant young warriors circling the waiting travelers. André was concerned completely for a moment with staying on his madly charging horse. Controlling the animal was out of the question. It was merely a matter of staying on until the madness subsided.

After a circle or two, the leaders of the welcoming party drew to a sliding stop before Red Feather. The others began to bunch behind, spreading informally to face the newcomers.

"*Ah-koh*, my chief," called a young warrior, in the semiformal greeting. "We have waited your coming."

"It is good," answered Red Feather. "Come, let us go!"

The meeting began to break up into an informal mixture. There were greetings between friends and relatives, laughter, excited talk, admiring comments about new horses or weapons.

André sat spellbound. He looked at Star, who was still caught up in the excitement of the occasion. Her white teeth gleamed through the dust on her face, and the net effect was one of sheer happiness.

"*Mon dieu!*" said Cartier at his elbow. "What a ride!"

He, too, had been caught up in the youthful exuberance of the celebration.

"Star, who are these men?" asked André.

She looked at him for a moment, a trifle puzzled.

"Nobody especially, Sky-Eyes. Just warriors from other bands who ride out to meet us. Come, I want to ask about my family."

They moved among the riders, Pale Star calling out to other horsemen.

"Southern band? Who is from the Southern band?"

A lithe young warrior reined in beside them, smiling broadly.

"I am," he announced.

"They are well?" Star asked eagerly.

"Yes. We wintered well."

In his face was an unspoken question. He looked at André and Cartier quizzically, but was too polite to inquire directly.

"Do you know the lodge of White Hawk?" Star asked.

"Of course. He is a great warrior."

"He is my father."

A look of disbelief crossed the young man's face.

"How are you called?"

"Pale Star."

"But you were stolen."

"Yes. Now I come back. This is my husband, Sky-Eyes, and his friend Woodchuck. Woodchuck is married to a girl of the Eastern band."

The young man nodded a greeting to the others.

"And you are Pale Star?"

"Of course. Are my parents well?"

"Yes, I think so. I saw them only yesterday."

"Tell me," she asked hesitantly, "my uncle, Looks Far. Is he still alive?"

"The medicine man? Ah, yes, he is as ever, skillful and respected."

Good. Star had worried about that. Looks Far was now a man of many winters. She had hoped that he could meet her husband, that the two might talk.

"Your family will be surprised to see you," the young man was saying. "They think you are dead."

"Sky-Eyes," said Star impulsively, "let us ride ahead."

André nodded, smiling.

"You wish me to guide you?" the young warrior asked.

"Yes. Are you ready?"

"Of course."

"Are you coming, Woodchuck?" called Star.

"No, go on," smiled the sergeant. "Cloud and I will stay with her people. We will see you tomorrow."

30

» » »

André sat on his horse, openmouthed in amazement. Spread before them were more lodges than he had ever seen before. The young warrior who had guided them spread a hand before him in a sweeping gesture of presentation.

"The People," he said simply.

"They are so many!" André gasped.

"Yes, Sky-Eyes," smiled the girl. "The People are strong, since we have had the horse."

"It was not always so?"

"No. My ancestor, Heads Off, brought the First Elk-dog."

"But where did he come from?"

"From the south, it is said."

André was confused. He was hearing of an ancient tribal legend, a story of an outsider who had come to the plains, bringing horses. Who or what had created this legend? And how had these primitive people become such proficient horsemen? There was much here that did not readily meet the eye.

"You must talk to Looks Far," Star was saying. "He will know much, and will answer your questions."

The little party moved down the hill toward the camp.

"There is the Sun Dance lodge." Their guide pointed.

It was a large arborlike structure, roofed with branches, and appeared nearly completed.

"The Elk-dog band is camped there," he continued. "To the west, the Red Rocks and the Mountain band. The Northern band against the slope there. Your Eastern band will camp here."

He pointed to a large open area apparently reserved for the latecomers.

"We are not of the Eastern band," said Pale Star quickly, a trifle irritated.

"Of course. Forgive me. You were only traveling with them."

The man chuckled.

André was puzzled by this exchange, as well as by the reserved area left for the approaching band.

"Tell me, Star, are camping places assigned?"

"No. Well, yes, in a way. Each band comes from a different direction, and that is their place in the circle."

"The circle?"

"Yes. It is the same in the Big Council. The chiefs of the Northern band sit to the north side of the circle, and so on around, our band to the south."

"But the Eastern band's place is not directly east."

"No. There must be an opening in the east side for the Sun. It is the same in the Big Council."

"A space is left for the sun?"

"Yes, and another space for the lost band. There were once six bands, but one was killed."

"Killed? When? By whom?"

"I do not know, Sky-Eyes," she said impatiently. "It was long ago. There is an empty spot in the Council circle for them, to the southeast. Ask Looks Far. Now come on!"

She touched heels to her horse, eager to rejoin her family. Of course, André thought. She would not want to make small talk about the tribe. Her activity was that of nervous anticipation. He followed her at a lope.

Star pulled her horse to a sliding stop before one of the larger skin lodges.

"White Hawk?" she called. "Spotted Fawn?"

The door-skin was pulled aside and a woman peered out with a puzzled frown.

"Yes? Who is it?"

"Mother! It is Pale Star! I have come home!"

The girl jumped from her horse and into the arms of the startled woman. There were joyous tears, everyone talked at once, and people came running from nearby lodges. White Hawk stepped out of the lodge and joined in the embrace.

"Child, we thought you were dead!"

"I did too, sometimes." Star laughed through the tears.

André sat waiting, watching the reunion. It was a strange feeling, to see his wife's parents for the first time. He had not known what to expect.

"Mother, Father, come here," Star was saying. "This is my husband, Sky-Eyes."

André stepped from his horse and strode forward. He was nervous and uncomfortable, unsure of what form of greeting would be expected. Should he shake hands?

"*Ah-koh,*" he said, with a little bowing nod.

"He speaks our tongue?" asked White Hawk.

"Only a little," answered André for himself. "A little sign-talk, too, my chief."

White Hawk studied the face of his new son-in-law closely.

"You can see to follow sign-talk?"

He waved a hand slowly in front of André's face.

"Of course, Father," laughed Star. "He can see as well as you."

"But his eyes—they are white!"

André was completely confused.

"What is it, Star?" he asked in French.

"My father has never seen blue eyes before," she explained, "except the clouded blue-white of a blind person. He thought you were blind."

She turned and explained in her own tongue. André found that he could follow fairly well.

"Among my husband's tribe," she began, "there are

many with eyes of different colors. They see equally well."

"*Aiee!*" murmured White Hawk softly. "What is his tribe?"

"They are called the *Fran-coy*. They come from across the Big Salty Water. Some have fur on the face."

"Is this the tribe of our ancestor?" Hawk asked in astonishment.

"I think not, Father. There are more than one tribe of Hairfaces."

There it was again, thought André. A reference to a hair-faced outsider who had joined the tribe long ago. What did it mean?

"Did you travel here alone?" Star's mother was asking.

"No, Mother. We were with Woodchuck, of my husband's tribe, and then with the Eastern band since they left the River of Swans. Sky-Eyes and I rode ahead."

"Then the Eastern band is near?"

"Oh yes, they will be here tonight."

"Is your friend Woodchuck with them?"

"Yes. He married a woman of the Eastern band."

There was a quiet, tolerant chuckle among the onlookers.

"The Eastern band is noted for foolish ways," Star explained quickly in French. "There are jokes about it."

"Jokes?"

"Yes. I will tell you more later. They have been more respected under Red Feather."

Star resumed her own tongue.

"Woodchuck's wife is the daughter of Red Feather."

There was an appreciative murmur, showing respect for the Eastern band's chief, and, in turn, for the outsider chosen by his daughter.

"Come, Star," White Hawk was saying. "Sit and tell us all that has happened since you were stolen. We tried to follow, but lost the trail."

"Yes, I know. What of the other children?"

"Of course! You did not know. They were ransomed back the next summer."

"Good! I will want to see them."

"Yes, but now tell us of your own travels."

They sat down, and Star began her story.

*   *   *

Much later, André snuggled with his wife in the buffalo robes. Across the dying fire, on the other side of the
lodge, slept Star's parents. He could hear their soft, regu-
lar breathing.

He had just heard the details of Star's abduction, her
time with Traveler and Plum Leaf, and her enslavement
by the crazed Three Owls. He had already known part of
the story, but not its entirety. How shocking, the things
he had learned!

His heart went out once more to this brave and resourceful young woman. Any trace of resentment for her having deceived the others of the party was now gone. Now
he only wanted to hold and protect her from the world
and its hazards.

Just as she had held and protected him, he realized,
from death in the watery grave of the churning river. He
held her closer.

"Thank you, Sky-Eyes," she whispered. "It is good."

31

» » »

*T*he Moon of Thunder, probably July by our calendar.
I have made an interesting dicovery about the People.
There is in their tradition a legend of an outsider, who is
said to have had facial hair. He is called Heads Off,
which origin is a mystery. Many prominent people in the
tribe trace their ancestry to this man. He is much re-
vered, though he became only a sub-chief, a leader of
one of the bands, long ago.

As a matter of interest, tradition also says that Heads
Off came from the south, and that he brought the first
horses.

André paused in his writing, and pondered for a little
while. There was little more to say for the present. Perhaps he should stop for now and finish the entry in his
journal when he had learned more.

He allowed the ink to dry, then carefully rewrapped
the packet. There was much he wished to know about
the People. Yes, and about this odd circumstance in their
history, that of the outsider. These warriors appeared

quite skilled with the horse. How many generations would
be required for the newly acquired horse to become the
basis for an entire buffalo-hunting culture?

He could tell that several generations had passed, because several families traced their ancestry to Heads Off.
And that name! It conjured up visions of a bloodthirsty
warrior, beheading his victims. This did not appear to be
the picture of this man, however. The tales of Heads Off
spoke of his wisdom and his skill with the horse, but not
of his violence. Even the story of the Great Battle, in
which Heads Off defeated an enemy chief in mortal combat, had no gruesome details. Clearly, something was
missing in the legend André was hearing. There must be
another reason for the name. Perhaps when he was able
to talk with Looks Far, the medicine man could answer
some of his questions. At least, Star had told him so. She
had gone to inquire when the meeting might take place.

André's thoughts were interrupted by Star's approach.

"Come, Sky-Eyes. Looks Far will talk with you now."

She led him among the lodges and stopped before one
with extensive painted decoration. It was not a large
dwelling, but somehow its appearance was imposing.
There was dignity in the geometric designs and symbols.

André paused. He had felt like this once when he had
been called before the headmaster at school over some
minor infraction. Now, however, the anticipation that
gnawed at his belly was of excitement, not fear.

"*Ah-koh*, Uncle," called Star. "I have brought my husband to talk to you."

A woman drew the door-skin aside and motioned them
to enter.

"No, no," said a man's voice, "we will talk outside."

André was pleased that he understood the phrase.

The medicine man stepped through the doorway and
straightened.

"*Ah-koh*," he said with a slight smile. "The day is
warm. Let us walk by the stream. How is it you are called?"

"I am Sky-Eyes, Uncle."

Star had taught him the use of this term to address any
adult male older than himself. It was a term of respect
and deference.

Looks Far nodded, pleased.

"You speak our language. Good."

"Only a little. Some sign-talk."

André felt that he was repeating himself at each new meeting.

"It is enough." The other nodded.

"Uncle," interrupted Star, "I go back to my mother's lodge. We will speak later."

"Of course." Looks Far smiled. "We will return."

He waved a hand at the departing girl. André paused to admire for a moment the lithe beauty of his wife's swinging stride. His thoughts were interrupted by the medicine man.

"I am grateful for your kindness to our daughter."

André paused a moment, not understanding the use of the term "daughter" by Star's uncle. Then he realized that, in this instance, the medicine man used it in the sense of a daughter of the tribe.

"It is nothing, Uncle. I am proud to be her husband."

Looks Far nodded, pleased.

"It is said you come from a far country?"

"Yes."

"Why do you come here?"

This direct question took André off guard for a moment. Looks Far was certainly direct and to the point. What was the man really asking?

"These are my wife's people."

"But this is not your only reason."

It was a statement, not a question. It was not an accusation, not unfriendly or prying, merely a statement.

André felt a trifle embarrassed. It was as if, somehow, this man could see right through to his soul. He struggled a moment to assure himself that he actually had no ulterior motive.

"Uncle," he said openly, "my chief sent me to find a water path to the west."

The medicine man paused in his stride and looked for a moment at his companion.

"Why?"

"To trade beyond the Big Water."

André expected another "why," but Looks Far only walked on. At last he spoke again.

"There is no water path to the west. There are mountains."

"I know that now. But it was what I came to find out."

He did not feel it necessary to explain that Pale Star had deceived them at first. He was surprised, almost, when Looks Far brought up the subject.

"But your wife knew."

"Yes, Uncle, but Star was not my wife then."

He surprised himself a little with his readiness to defend the girl. Looks Far nodded solemnly, and André felt a great depth of understanding and approval.

A few months ago, he would have doubted that he could respect the wisdom of any of the natives as he was now beginning to respect this man. The dignity, the demeanor of the medicine man was that of a philosopher, a teacher. André found himself eager to learn.

"Pale Star tells me that you have found the spirit of the grassland," Looks Far said tentatively.

"I do not know, Uncle," André began honestly. "There is much I would learn. This is very different from my own country."

"Yet you find happiness here."

"Of course. It is the land of my wife's people."

Looks Far nodded approvingly.

"Yet, Sky-Eyes, I am made to feel that it is more. Your spirit mixes well with the spirit of the prairie."

"Its spirit? Does a place have a spirit, Uncle?"

Looks Far glanced at the young man curiously.

"All things have spirits, my son. Do you not feel this?"

André felt a strange prickling sensation at the back of his neck. He had never spoken of these things to anyone. Here he was, in the middle of an unexplored continent, discussing philosophy with an illiterate savage. Still, he felt the wisdom of the other. Somehow, he felt that with all his formal schooling in the academies of Europe, he was the uneducated one here.

"You must understand, Uncle, that in my country this is not—"

He paused, confused. He had almost said "known." How strange that he had nearly become apologetic for the backwardness of modern culture. He fumbled for words to express himself.

"—is not considered important," he finished lamely.

Looks Far seemed to overlook the embarrassment of the other. He only nodded in understanding.

"That is unfortunate."

Now there came flooding into André's memory the theories of Calvin and of Rabelais. What an opportunity to discuss with this wise teacher the basic goodness of man.

"Uncle, some of our teachers say that man is good, but falls into evil with greed. Others that he is bad and must rise above it. What is the teaching of your people?"

The medicine man looked at him in astonishment.

"Your people are troubled by such things?"

"Yes, maybe so." André felt apologetic again.

Looks Far strolled for a few moments before he answered. He stared at a band of grazing horses in the stream's bend, herded by a couple of youths.

"Men are like horses," he mused. "None are all good or all bad. There is good and bad in all, some more than others, or at different times."

How simple it seemed, when voiced by Looks Far. André began to appreciate why Star held this man almost in reverence.

Another thought occurred to him.

"Uncle, would you tell me of your forefather, Heads Off?"

Again Looks Far gave him that quick, quizzical look, a mixture of surprise, wonder, and approval.

"Of course, Sky-Eyes. I will show you the Story Skins."

"Story Skins?"

"Yes, the story of the People, painted on skins. I will show you."

32

» » »

André sat on a pile of robes, waiting. Overhead, hanging from the lodgepoles, were bunches and bundles of herbs, twigs, and drying flowers. The plants gave forth a pungent sagelike odor, new yet vaguely familiar. He had no idea as to their purpose, but was increasingly impressed with the medicine man's expertise.

Outside at the summer cooking fire, Blue Dawn, wife of Looks Far, busied herself with food preparation.

Looks Far rummaged behind the lodge lining, among the accoutrements of his profession, and drew forth several long cylinders of rolled skin.

"Yes," he murmured, "this one."

He untied the thongs that held it, and carefully, almost reverently, spread the skin on the ground between them.

André watched, fascinated. The skin was completely covered with pictographs. Some were of people, animals, some of fire or rain.

"This is the story of the People," Looks Far was explaining. "There is one picture for each year. The pictures start in the middle and move out in a circle."

He indicated with a forefinger the direction of the spiral.

André was astonished. Here, in the absence of a written language, was an attempt to record the history of the tribe. This skin alone must have thirty or forty pictographs.

"Who draws the pictures?" André asked.

"The medicine man. See, here the pictures change. This begins the time of my grandfather Owl."

He pointed to an obvious difference in artistic technique.

"Does he decide what to put in the picture?"

"Sometimes. It is supposed to be some important event of that season. See, this is the Year We Ate the Horses."

He pointed to a scene where emaciated people were skinning and butchering a dead horse.

"But, Uncle, tell me of Heads Off."

"Ah, yes. Here."

He pointed to a pictograph of a man on a horse.

"See, before this there are no elk-dogs."

It was true. In the inner curls of the spiral on the story-skin there were no horses. This was the first.

"This is my ancestor, Heads Off," Looks Far said solemnly. "He rides the First Elk-dog."

André peered closely. The man appeared to have a black beard.

"He had hair on the face?" he asked.

"Yes. He was called Hair-Face by our enemies."

"But why, Uncle, why was he called Heads Off?"

Looks Far smiled and shrugged.

"I do not know, Sky-Eyes. My grandfather said it was a joke. When he first came to the People he seemed to take his head off."

André studied the picture again, and moved on to the next. In it, the same man appeared, now with other mounted men. They appeared to be driving loose horses. In the next, they were hunting buffalo on horseback, with lances. Then came a striking picture of hand-to-hand combat, with the same bearded man killing his opponent. A line connected the defeated enemy to a small picture of a dog or wolf.

"What is this?" asked André.

"That is the Great Battle. Heads Off killed the enemy chief Gray Wolf."

Then the young man noticed a curious thing. In the first picture, Heads Off appeared different somehow. His head was larger, and smoothly rounded. Could it be?

"Uncle," he asked, "could he be wearing a helmet?"

There was a moment of confusion while the two attempted to find a word with mutual understanding. "Head-dress" seemed to suffice.

Of course, thought André excitedly. The newcomer was a white man, wearing a military helmet. When he removed it, he appeared to take off his head. André attempted to explain his theory to Looks Far.

"Yes," admitted the medicine man cautiously. "It maybe was a headdress."

Now excited over the implications, André asked more questions.

"He brought the horses?"

"Yes, and the Elk-dog medicine to control them."

"He taught the People?"

"Yes, but more. He brought the medicine."

"I do not understand."

"Here. I will show you."

Looks Far rose and reached up to take down an object from the dim upper portion of the lodge. There was a metallic jingle as he sat back down and displayed it in his hands.

André could hardly grasp the significance. It was an iron bit, a ring bit with silver dangles that tinkled and sparkled in the light. Tiny ornamental silver chains looped below the shanks of the bit.

It seemed strangely out of place, in this primitive land whose people had no metallic tools at all, to see this familiar object. The style and pattern were unmistakable.

"Uncle," he stammered, "when did Heads Off come?"

"Who knows? Long ago. We have had the horse for many seasons."

The passage of time, André had noticed before, meant little to these people. Anything beyond a generation was "a long time ago." With no clocks or timepieces of any sort, time's passage had simply never become important. Years were tallied on the Story Skins, but even that had no important use. It was more of a recognition of past deeds than a record of time.

"You mentioned your grandfather?"

"Yes, he was called Owl. He was a son of Heads Off."

Ah, thought André. This allows a count of the generations. Looks Far, well past middle age, is the great-grandson. This could easily mean nearly a century since the outsider came to them.

He was only beginning to realize the great changes that the horse must have brought. Now their entire life revolved around the hunting of buffalo.

"Uncle, before the horse, how did the People hunt?"

Looks Far smiled, a sad, tired smile.

"That is before my memory, Sky-Eyes, but I was told as a child. It was very hard, and there were times of starvation."

He pointed to the older portions of the Story Skin, the inner curls of the spiral. Hunters were depicted hiding in wait with weapons ready. In one picture, buffalo seemed to be falling over a precipice.

"What does that mean, Uncle?"

"Ah, that was a great story. Long ago, a great medicine man named White Buffalo called a herd to him, and the hunters drove them over the bluff. It was a great kill."

"He *called* them?"

"Yes, Sky-Eyes. A young medicine man still learns this skill."

"But how can this be?"

The older man shrugged.

"It is something that takes many seasons in the learning. He must learn to get inside the buffalo's head, to share its spirit."

This was becoming more complicated than André could grasp. He retreated to more secure ground.

"The Elk-dog medicine—it is used in the horse's mouth?"

"Oh no. Heads Off used it so, of course. Now it is only used for ceremony. But it is very strong medicine."

André nodded. How strange that this article of common use had become almost a religious talisman for the People.

"It was stolen by our enemies once," Looks Far was continuing. "My father journeyed all the way to the mountains in the northwest to recover it."

André found himself hungering to hear more of this remarkable story, but the shadows were growing long. He must not intrude on the hospitality of these people.

"I must return to my wife's family," he stated formally. "May we talk again?"

"Of course, my son."

André left the lodge of the medicine man elated at all he had learned, yet wishing to know more. He could hardly wait to record in his journal some of this astounding information.

It was next morning before he was able to find a time and place alone for the purpose.

I have learned much about these natives since last I took pen in hand. Their history, though crudely recorded, indicates Spanish contact nearly a century ago. This explains their expert use of the horse.

One of the revered objects of the tribe is a Spanish bit, which was used in the mouth of the first horse ever seen by these natives. It is believed to contain the power by which horses are controlled. Its owner, an important figure in their heritage, was undoubtedly a Spaniard.

It seems a mystery why Spain has not followed this first contact with settlement. This is a rich and noble land, ripe for colonization. These natives are friendly, and could be dealt with profitably.

It seems a clear mandate for us to colonize in the name of His Majesty King Louis.

33
» » »

The Sun Dance was over now, the Big Council had met, deliberated, and dispersed. It was time for the bands to go their separate ways.

With this came a time of decision for André and Cartier as well. They had discussed the alternatives briefly. Neither had overwhelming sentiments about it.

Their primary duty, of course, lay in their mission, but that had been negated by failure. By all standard protocol, they should now return as quickly as possible to report their negative findings.

However, it was easy to convince themselves otherwise. They had learned much about this unexplored land, and were learning more. This would prove invaluable when colonization began. So, they assured each other, they should learn as much as possible before returning to Fort Mishi-ghan.

"We should be able to report the distance to the mountains," André assured the sergeant. "There may also be Spanish forts."

Cartier nodded in agreement.

"Pale Star says that the Mountain and Red Rocks bands will go there," André continued.

"To the Spanish?"

"No, to the mountains."

"Did you ask if they would take us?"

"No, not yet. Cartier, did you know it is customary for the husband to join his wife's band?"

The sergeant shrugged.

"Yes, it is usual, I am told. But, Lieutenant, we have our mission."

"I know. We must complete that, and still not offend the customs of the People, if it can be avoided. Of course, we could simply leave the girls when we are ready."

André saw instantly that he had struck a nerve with that thrust. Cartier fidgeted a moment, looking at the ground, before he spoke.

"Lieutenant," he said slowly, "I did not think of this as a temporary arrangement. Cloud is my wife, not my mistress."

"Of course. It is the same with me, my friend. I only wished to be sure. Now let us ask Star to answer some of our questions."

Pale Star quickly understood the dilemma that the men faced. She had wondered, too, about their course of action, and was ready with information and suggestions.

"It is too late in the season to start back to Mishighan, Sky-Eyes."

He nodded. This much seemed apparent.

"How far to the mountains?"

"Maybe one moon."

A month, André pondered. It was now early July, as nearly as he could calculate. To travel there and back would place them back in this area in September or October. He had little knowledge of the climate here.

"When does winter come?"

There was a moment of confusion while they attempted to sort out words for "frost" and "snow."

"Cold sometimes in the Moon of Falling Leaves," Star told him. "Cold Maker comes to stay in the Moon of Long Nights."

That would be December, André decided.

"Then we could travel three, maybe four more moons?"

"Yes. You wish to see the mountains?"

André nodded tentatively.

"Sky-Eyes, here is a plan. We could go with the Red Rocks band, and then return to winter in my father's lodge."

"There is time?"

"Yes."

"How will we know where to find them?"

Star smiled.

"You still do not understand a tribe that moves from one camp to another. We ask them where they are going."

It sounded so simple when she explained it. André felt a little foolish.

Another question occurred to him.

"What about Pink Cloud? She would wish to be with her people."

"Yes. But I have talked with her. She knows that Woodchuck must have loyalty to you, as his chief."

Star paused and giggled softly.

"I think she wants to go on this adventure. She will see her parents again next spring."

Thoughts of the next season brought another concern to André's mind.

"Star, you know we must return to Mishi-ghan someday."

There was a hint of sadness in the dark eyes for just a moment. Then she brightened.

"Yes, of course. But it cannot be this season. Besides, your chief said to stay as long as we need. We can think about that later."

André was uneasy with her answer. For the first time, he wondered. Would there come a day when she would leave him to stay with her own people? He would rather not think about it now.

No sooner had that gloomy premonition flitted through his mind than Star smiled at him. Instantly, all doubts and fears vanished. Her smile could right every wrong, remove all doubts.

"It is good." He smiled in return. "Now, should we ask someone if we can travel with them?"

"It is not a thing we *must* do," she pondered, "but it would be good. Come, we will talk to the chief of the Red Rocks."

She jumped to her feet and started away.

"Their home is nearer than that of the Mountain band," she said over her shoulder. "Our travel will be shorter."

"But they do go to the mountains?" André hurried his steps to keep up with her long stride.

"Yes. The Mountain band goes farther north. Both will winter in the shadow of the mountains, but the Red Rocks nearly straight west of here."

"The mountains lie north and south?"

Star only nodded.

André was beginning to grasp the general conformation of the country. A broad plain, bordered by mountains in a range to the west. He could draw a better map today, he mused, than the one in Le Blanc's office. His mission would result in some good, after all. He would be helping to map the uncharted wilderness.

Star stopped in front of one of the more pretentious lodges in the Red Rocks area and spoke to a dignified man reclining on a willow backrest.

"*Ah-koh*, my chief. I am Pale Star, of the Elk-dogs, and this is my husband, Sky-Eyes."

The old chief nodded, waiting. He was probably well aware of the presence of the newcomers in the encampment.

"My chief," began André formally, "we would travel with you to the west."

The chief took a long pull at his pipe before answering. Finally he spoke for the first time.

"Why?"

André felt that he had lived this conversation before. Now, however, his goals were different, and he was more experienced in the native ways.

"I wish to see new places, and to learn more of the land of my wife's people."

The old man looked at him for the space of several heartbeats.

"It is good," he said finally. "We will leave tomorrow."

André nodded.

"There is another thing," Star interjected. "Woodchuck, of my husband's tribe, would go with us too. His wife is—"

"Ah, yes, the daughter of Red Feather." The chief nodded. "It is good."

It seemed that this band chief was quite well informed.

"We will be ready, my chief," Star assured him.

34

>> >> >>

The two Frenchmen sat on their horses, waiting. If their families had chanced to see them, it is doubtful whether they would have even recognized them, André thought.

Both were dressed in the buckskin garments of the People and wore their distinctive pattern of footwear. In addition, their hair had grown long. For convenience, both men had elected to braid it in the fashion of the People. With the help of their wives, they had learned the skill required to present an acceptable appearance.

They had been well accepted by the Red Rocks band, especially since they had joined in the hunts. The addition of two young warriors to the strength of the band was welcomed.

André had chosen the lance as his favorite weapon. He had excelled with it in the academy, and its use for buffalo was a logical progression. He could ride up behind a fleeing buffalo, approaching from the left, and place his lance behind the rib cage with unerring skill.

This had quickly earned him the respect of the other warriors.

Cartier, on the other hand, had continued his progress with the bow. Soon he could ride and shoot from horseback quite accptably.

Just now, they were waiting to take part in one last big hunt of the season. It was the Moon of the Hunter, and they must leave soon to return to the Elk-dog band.

Mid-October, André believed. The leaves of the cottonwoods had changed from green to bright yellow almost overnight. Now most of them had fallen. Nights were crisp and clear, the days warm and fragrant with the spicy smells of autumn. It was a pleasant time to be alive.

André had not written in his journal for some time. Somehow it seemed unimportant when compared to relaxing with Star or riding to hunt buffalo under the bluest skies he had ever seen. High overhead, long lines of geese honked their way south for the season.

André could see mountains in the distance, lying blue along the horizon. He would have loved to ride toward them, but it seemed impractical. That blue haze was many sleeps away, Star assured him. The Red Rocks would move much closer before making permanent winter camp. Just now, they were camped on the plain to hunt until their stores were sufficient. That, or until winter howled down on them, whichever came sooner.

"Ah! He comes!" The man on André's left spoke softly.

A scout had been working ahead, evaluating the best approach to the hunt. The herd was scattered widely across the prairie.

The scout beckoned to the waiting hunters.

"There is a small band, maybe forty, in a little basin there." He pointed. "We can circle through this gully, around that hill, and spread out. We will be downwind. *Aiee*, it will go well."

In a short while, the hunters were arrayed in a long line facing the distant buffalo. They would walk slowly until the herd became disturbed, then charge forward.

Horses were becoming skittish, eager to plunge ahead.

André quieted his horse with a hand on her neck. They walked on.

"Slowly, now, little mare," he crooned.

An old cow raised her head to sniff the air, found nothing amiss, and resumed eating. André marveled once more at the poor eyesight of the creatures. They could be approached within a few hundred paces if the hunter remained downwind.

Now another animal paced restlessly. The muffled sound of many horses' hooves must be creating some uneasiness. A cow called softly to her calf. A yearling bull trotted aimlessly, head up, peering to see beyond the range of his nearsighted vision.

The hunters were as close as a long bow-shot when the break came. As if by a signal, the herd wheeled to run. They pounded across the meadow and clattered through the stony bed of a dry wash, with the horsemen in hot pursuit.

Someone voiced the full-throated war cry of the People. It was not a legitimate part of the hunt, but an uncontrollable expression of excitement. André found himself yelling too.

The horsemen drew closer, and André saw a buffalo stumble and fall. To his right, Cartier urged his horse forward, coming alongside a running animal to draw his bow. The buffalo fell, and the sergeant reached for another arrow.

André selected a target and lowered his lance point. At the shock of contact, the well-trained buffalo horse squatted on her heels in a sliding stop. The momentum of the dying buffalo freed the lance and André kneed the mare forward again, searching for another kill.

The hunt was over very quickly. Warriors moved among the fallen buffalo, administering a final blow or arrow to the wounded. Men were beginning to call to friends, laughing and congratulating each other on the success of the effort. More than thirty carcasses lay strewn on the grass.

"A good day, Sky-Eyes," someone called. "Your lance does well."

André waved in acknowledgment and looked around

for Cartier. There was an exhilaration in the air, a pride in a job well done. It was good to be praised by one's colleagues, he noted.

The sergeant rode up, a broad grin on his face.

"How many?" André greeted him. "I saw one fall."

"Three!" chortled Cartier. *"Mon dieu*, a man could come to like this work!"

André chuckled. It seemed impossible that a few months ago both had been civilized military men, professional soldiers. Here they were, participating in a buffalo kill with natives, halfway across the continent. Participating *as* natives, he told himself with wonder. Their purpose was to provide food for themselves and others for the lean months of the coming winter.

Not only that, they were using native weapons with stone points. What a story to tell on their return to civilization!

Oddly, their return seemed unimportant now. The warm hazy days of autumn lay across the prairie like a comforting hand, soothing the senses. Everything seemed in tune, with themselves and the People in harmony with the world.

35

» » »

"**L**ieutenant, I would talk with you."

Cartier seemed serious. His usually jovial face was sober.

"Of course. What is it, Woodchuck?"

They had easily fallen into the habit of calling each other by the names the natives had given them. It was simpler. Now, André realized, the sergeant must have something very serious on his mind, to address him as Lieutenant.

André leaned forward on his willow backrest and drew on the pipe he was smoking. It was a relaxing thing, the pipe. When he had first tried it, his chest burned, he coughed violently, and a row of tiny dragons seemed intent on chewing the edges of his tongue.

Now he had perfected the technique, and found the aromatic smoke of mixed leaves quite pleasant. He was particularly fond of the spicy smell of sumac when mixed with tobacco.

Cartier heaved a deep sigh and dropped to a squatting position. They had also adopted this mannerism. In a civilization with no chairs, one must assume the customs of the natives. The Frenchmen had found the odd posture comfortable once they became used to it. Now Cartier sat easily on his heels to continue the conversation.

"Lieutenant," he began, his brow furrowed with concern, "we must make a decision."

"And what is that, my friend?"

André was comfortable, relaxed, and in the warm autumn sunlight, decisions seemed unimportant. Cartier stiffened a little, and André thought he detected a slight irritation in the other's face. The sergeant seemed so troubled, so aloof. With it, whatever the problem might be, came a return to the military formality that they had almost abandoned.

The sergeant rose, perhaps confused by this conflict of cultures. He stood in a military position "at ease," with hands clasped behind him.

"Begging the Lieutenant's pardon, sir, but we are on a military assignment."

"Yes, Sergeant?"

Now André was a trifle irritated. Was the man trying to tell him his duty? He waited.

Cartier's face flushed with embarrassment.

"Sir," he almost stammered, "should we not think of going back?"

"Back to Mishi-ghan? Sergeant, we have discussed this. There is not time this season."

"No, sir. I mean, back to the other bands. To your wife's people, or mine."

"Oh. But tell me, why is this so important?"

Inwardly, André knew it was important. He only wished to avoid decisions just now.

"Perhaps it is not, sir," Cartier said stiffly. "I only thought that if we are to winter with the other bands, our travel time is growing short."

"You are right, Sergeant. It is important."

"Yes, sir. The Red Rocks move to the mountains in three more days. Do we go with them?"

"They do? I mean, they will? How do you know this?"

"It was decided this morning. Cloud told me."

"I see. Then we must decide."

"Yes, sir. Lieutenant, there is one more thing: My wife is pregnant."

Ah, thought André, so that was it. Cartier has been concerned for his wife's well-being.

"I see. What does she suggest?"

"Nothing, sir. She will do as we decide."

Cartier paused, somewhat embarrassed, and then continued.

"Lieutenant, I know little of such things, but in another month or two she will be in mid-pregnancy. Would it be wise to be traveling with winter coming on?"

"I don't know either. Probably not."

"If it were not for the pregnancy, Lieutenant, she could—"

"Yes, yes, my friend. I understand. Let us ask the girls."

In the end it was Pale Star who suggested an obvious compromise.

"We can winter with the Red Rocks. You wish to see the mountains, and write more in your talking book. Then we will join the other bands at the Big Council in the summer."

"But we have no lodge."

Pale Star smiled.

"Sky-Eyes, many people have been helped by your buffalo kills and those of Woodchuck. They will help us make a lodge cover, and cut poles. The four of us can live together."

André quickly saw that it was now easier to rationalize what he had really wanted all along. He could explore the front range of the distant mountains and chart their position for future expeditions.

"Is Cloud willing to do this?"

"Yes, Sky-Eyes. It is an easier and shorter journey than to return to her people. The Eastern band will winter at the River of Swans, which is far away."

It was decided that simply. Star and Cloud started to spread the word that they would be staying and would need a lodge. Since the Frenchmen had given away most of their kills, many people responded with help. A skin from here, another from there, one from someone else.

A young warrior who had become a close friend offered the loan of a horse and two lodgepoles to use as a pole-drag. They would be needed to transport the partially completed lodge cover. Others promised help when the band reached the winter camp site.

André was elated. This would work well for their mission, now modified again. For the first time in many days, he took out his journal to record this turn of events.

The Moon of Falling Leaves, probably October. Since there is little time for travel before cold weather, we have elected to winter with the Red Rocks band of these people. They will camp, we are told, against the mountains. This should provide an excellent opportunity for exploration and evaluation with the prospect of settlement.

He paused in thought for some time, uncertain whether to pursue the theme. Then he turned back to his pen.

I will continue the ledger after some exploration has taken place. Meanwhile, I will begin a map of the area which will aid the first incoming settlers.

It should be noted that these natives are extremely hospitable, and are helping us provision for the winter.

André turned to a fresh sheet and began a rough map, with Mishi-ghan in the upper right of the page. He sketched in the Big River on which they had traveled and its major junction, where their canoes had been destroyed. He roughed in an estimate of the portion of the River of Swans which they had encountered. Then he turned the page to a new angle and carefully lettered "mountains" along its left margin. He would add more detail later.

Meticulously, he rewrapped the packet and returned it to his pocket. Then he hurried to assist in the preparation for the move.

36
» » »

It was the Moon of Greening again. The Red Rocks band had wintered well. Even the Moon of Hunger had presented little hunger. Supplies had been adequate.

André's wife had told him of a saying of the People that the Moon of Hunger needs a new name.

"Looks Far says that before we had elk-dogs, there was much starvation."

André nodded.

"I saw the Story Skins."

They watched a long line of geese beat their way northward, honking as they went. A strange, primitive restlessness stirred in the depths of his being.

It seemed impossible that only a year ago the expedition to find the Southwest Water Passage had set out. Yet, in another way, it was a lifetime.

The two Frenchmen had adapted themselves to the culture of the People. There was little to do in the long days and nights of winter, so they did as others did. A number of people would gather in one of the larger lodges, to smoke and tell stories and gamble with the plum

155

stones. The guests had been welcome in these pastimes, but had avoided the gambling. They had little of value to gamble.

Woodchuck continued to whittle and carve, giving away most of the resulting items. He continued to be popular with the children, and a few loyal followers began to try to learn his craft.

Best of all, to André, were the story sessions. Pale Star was an acknowledged master at stories and could keep an audience spellbound for an entire evening. Others told stories too, and Star translated for the Frenchmen when necessary. It was no longer very necessary. They had rapidly acquired a working understanding of the tongue of the People.

There came a time when André was invited to tell his stories.

"I cannot do that, Star," he protested in French.

"Oh yes," she smiled. "I will translate."

"But what stories? Will they be offended if I do not do this?"

"No, but it will be big medicine if you do. Tell your Creation story."

André was uneasy. He recalled the first time he had seen this girl, exchanging stories with the missionary.

"Go ahead," she insisted. "Then someone will tell ours."

"You mean about Adam and Eve?"

"Yes. It is a good story."

"Well, I will try."

He turned and faced the group, seated and smoking around the fire.

"My friends," he began, "you know that Woodchuck and I come from far away. I will tell you how our people came to be."

There were nods of approval.

"In the beginning," he started, "the Great Father made the heavens and the earth."

There were eager nods. He continued, with little help from Star. By the time he got to the seventh day, when the Great Father rested, the audience was fascinated, and André was enjoying it. He continued on with Adam and

Eve, the Garden (which presented some translation difficulty), and the serpent. There was an approving murmur.

"See?" Star whispered. "It is good."

"It is good!" one of the listeners echoed. "Hear, now, the story of the People. Once we lived in the center of the earth, and never came outside. But then the Old Man came and sat on a hollow log, and tapped it with a stick. Out came First Man and First Woman."

Had it really been only a year since he had first heard this story, from the lips of the woman who now sat beside him as his wife?

"Then more people came out," continued the speaker, "and yet more."

"Are they still coming out?" asked Sergeant Cartier from across the fire.

"Of course not," answered the speaker indignantly. "The world would be full of people. They were stopped long ago when a fat woman got stuck in the log."

The listeners roared with laughter.

"That is part of the story," Star whispered in André's ear. "They try to get some stranger to ask that question."

The story session ended, and they moved out of the lodge to return to their various homes.

"Sky-Eyes," a man said to him as they parted, "I liked your story. That part about the snake is good."

He chuckled as he moved on.

Somehow, André felt more in tune, more a part of the People, after they had exchanged stories of origin. He became a favorite storyteller through the winter, with the help of Star.

André was well-read, and called on his memory of Greek mythology for material. Homer's poetic stories of the Trojan war came to life again for the listeners. The story of the Trojan horse was a favorite.

"They hid *inside* this elk-dog, Sky-Eyes?"

"Yes, Lean Bear. It was very large."

"*Aiee!*"

Spring had finally come. Birds were migrating and André was restless. He felt it now, as he stood with Star and watched the geese honk their way north. He was not sure what he wanted to do about it, and wondered if Star too felt the urgency in the air. He thought so.

"We will move soon, Sky-Eyes," she said in answer to his unspoken question.

"Where?"

"East, and onto the plain. The buffalo will return."

There was a shout, and they turned to see Cartier climbing toward them. He looked as if something had gone wrong.

"Star!" he blurted. "Cloud wants you to come! Her time is here."

Star nodded.

"It is good. I go!"

The two men stood looking at each other for a moment, and then both broke into nervous smiles.

"My friend, you are about to become a father!" André chided.

"Sky-Eyes, I am not sure I am ready for this."

"It will go well, Woodchuck."

"Of course. But this is different. This is *my* wife, Lieutenant."

It was still not easy for Cartier to forget military protocol, especially under stress.

"I understand, my friend. I, too, would be concerned. Come, we will go down."

"No, we cannot. Cloud said we must wait."

"Yes, we will wait outside, Woodchuck, but nearby."

It seemed a long time that they squatted or sat, just outside the camp, and waited for some word from their lodge. Finally, they saw the door-skin move, and Star came outside and straightened. She motioned to them and ducked back inside the lodge.

Woodchuck approached at a trot, followed by André. They entered the lodge and stood a moment to allow their eyes to adjust to the dim interior. Pink Cloud lay on her bed, covered with a light robe against the chill of the coming night. In the crook of her arm, contentedly nestled to her breast, lay the child.

"He is a fine boy, my husband." She smiled. "He will be a great hunter and warrior."

"You are all right, Cloud?" the sergeant mumbled.

"Of course, Woodchuck. Look, I am flat in front."

She lay a hand on her belly.

Cartier nodded.

"And the child is well formed?"

"No, better than that."

She turned so that the tiny face could be seen more easily.

"Look, he has your cheeks already. I will call him Ground Squirrel, the little Woodchuck, until time to name him."

"And when is that, Mother?" asked André.

"His second summer."

"Two years, by your count," Star interceded. "It is at his First Dance."

He said nothing, but André wondered to himself. Where would they be by the time of this child's naming?

37

» » »

It was the Moon of Growing, and the winter-tired band could hardly wait to move out onto the awakening prairie. The buffalo would be returning, Star assured her husband. The first hunt of the season would be a time of excitement.

The prospect of fresh meat, after weeks of dried meat and pemmican, was enough to make his mouth water. He could empathize with those who spoke with longing of the taste of fresh liver.

After the move, it was still several days before the coming of the buffalo. The scouts reported only scattered antelope, an occasional elk, and a few wild horses.

A couple of hunters from the band made an elk kill and shared the fresh meat. However, the council met and decreed that there must be no more such free-lance hunting until after the buffalo returned. Such activity might well frighten away the herds, causing them to move elsewhere.

It was a joyous day when an excited scout rode in with the good news.

"They come! The buffalo are coming!"

The leaders of the hunt had already been chosen, and they rode out to observe the terrain. The others waited impatiently. It was nearly dusk when the three sub-chiefs returned.

"It is good!" their leader reported to the anxious hunters. "There should be a good hunt. We will start at dawn."

The crowd scattered to make final preparations. For many, there would be little sleep tonight. Weapons would be checked and rechecked, prayers would be offered, and prized buffalo horses would be carefully readied for the hunt.

"Sky-Eyes, we would go, too," stated Pale Star, her dark eyes glistening with the excitement of the occasion.

André had almost ceased to be startled at the volatile nature of his wife, but this caught him by surprise. He recalled her excited participation in the horseback celebration of the previous summer. However, she had said "we."

"Who?"

"Cloud and I."

"But, Star, the baby is only a moon of age."

"Yes. That is why Cloud needs the change. She will leave the child with Badger Woman. We will not hunt, Sky-Eyes, only watch. Then we will be there already for the butchering."

It seemed logical when she explained it. André knew that women sometimes did join in the hunt. In fact, he had seen Pale Star make a buffalo kill with a bow and arrows last season. This time the women did not even intend that. They would watch from a safe vantage point, merely as a welcome escape from the routine of camp.

"It is good," he nodded. "Let us find your horses."

So it happened that when the hunters rode out to meet the dawning day, both Cloud and Star joined the party. As they approached the herd, Star reined in.

"We will wait here," she called. "Good hunting!"

Their husbands waved acknowledgment and moved on with the hunters.

"Your wife does well, my friend," André remarked to Cartier.

"Yes," responded the sergeant proudly, "she does. And do you see how the baby grows? Already he smiles, no?"

André chuckled to himself. Rarely had he seen so proud a father. He looked back and waved to the two women on the rise behind them. He and Cartier had both been fortunate to find such wives. For a moment the memory of Babette, the little flirt, crossed his mind. Her silly coquettishness seemed a part of another world, one he scarcely missed now. He had to remind himself that he and Cartier must soon return to Mishi-ghan with their report. Even that past seemed a lifetime away.

The scouts ahead now signaled a halt, and the hunt leader quickly pointed directions for deployment of the hunters. In a long line, they crossed the ridge and began the approach.

It was a good hunt, an exciting one. There was one strike that André missed when the fat yearling turned unexpectedly. That miss was offset somewhat by a lucky thrust at another animal.

Cartier was systematically pumping arrows into one buffalo after another. He was really becoming quite adept.

The herd swept on, out of the hunt area, and the hunters turned to guide the butchering parties to the proper kills. André and Cartier rode back toward the hillock where they had left the women, laughing and joking, still excited from the hunt.

Star and Cloud were urging their horses forward to meet them.

"Ours are the greatest of hunters!" shouted Star excitedly.

It was at that moment that André saw the creature lurch forward. From a patch of brush beside the place where the girls rode, a gigantic buffalo bull stumbled to his feet.

They were perhaps fifty paces away, but some things were etched permanently in the memory of the two men. The wounded bull, an arrow protruding from his flank, the bloody froth flying from his nose and mouth as he tossed his huge head. The sheer, irrational madness in the piggy little eyes as they focused on the enemy. There was but one motive evident in every fiber of the animal's being: absolute destruction of his tormentors as he charged.

"Look out!" screamed André.

Cartier was already pounding forward, but it was useless. Pink Cloud, riding nearest the bull's last hiding place, caught the onslaught of his fury. Her pony screamed in pain and terror as glistening black horns punched into its soft underbelly. Horse and girl were lifted high into the air to slam back to earth. Cloud was partly pinned beneath her dying horse, kicking frantically to free herself while the bull continued to worry his fallen foes.

Star was unarmed except for a knife, and circled to try for a thrust. Cartier slid his horse to a stop, at the same moment loosing an arrow behind the bull's ribs.

The animal whirled at this new tormentor and made an attempt to charge once more. His life was ebbing fast, and he stumbled and fell, bleeding from nose and mouth.

Both Star and Cartier jumped from their horses and ran to Pink Cloud. André paused a moment for one last lance thrust, and the buffalo lay still.

The three of them managed to extricate the girl from under the fallen horse.

"Is she all right?" André panted.

"I am afraid not, Sky-Eyes," Star said quietly in French. "See, she is badly crushed."

Cartier sat down and took her head in his lap, crying and rocking softly in his grief. His wife looked up into his usually cheerful face and managed a wan smile. Her face was ashen.

"I am sorry, my husband."

"We will take care of you," he protested. "You will see."

"No, no, Woodchuck. Only, stay here with me."

"Of course."

"Star? Come here."

The voice was hardly more than a whisper now.

"Take care of my baby?"

"Yes, Cloud. It will be so."

"Wait, Cloud," murmured Cartier helplessly. "Don't—"

But the eyes were losing their expression, and the ragged breathing was becoming more shallow. Then he felt her muscles relax, and the next breath did not come at all.

38

>> >> >>

Pink Cloud was buried in the custom of her people, on an elevated burial scaffold. The songs of mourning were sung for three days, and then the People resumed the ways of the living.

It was not to be for the three surviving friends. This tragedy had completely changed the lives of them all. André was puzzled as to how it would be possible to feed the motherless infant. In his own country, there would have been milk cows or goats. Here, there were none. Likewise, it seemed unlikely that any nursing mother could spare enough milk to support an extra child.

Star explained that some nourishment could be supplied by chewing meat until it was soft and then feeding it to the child.

"Will that be enough?"

"I do not know, Sky-Eyes," the girl answered solemnly.

Meanwhile the baby continued to scream hungrily. It seemed a hopeless task.

It was while tending the horses that André was struck by an idea. He hurried back to the lodge, returned with a waterskin, and roped an old mare. Clumsily, he began to squeeze the mare's milk into the narrow opening of the leather flask. At first he spilled most of it, but his technique improved rapidly. Before long, he had perhaps half a cup of fluid in the bag. He released the mare.

"Thank you, Mother. If this works, we will be back."

Back at the lodge, he pricked a small hole with a knife point at a corner of the water flask. He offered it to the crying infant. The baby grasped eagerly, then shook its head in frustration at the unfamiliar texture. In a moment, however, his eyes widened in surprise as the rich warm fluid began to flow.

"He takes it! It is good, Sky-Eyes!"

Scarcely pausing for breath, the baby gulped down the entire contents of the skin, belched noisily, and fell asleep in Pale Star's arms.

"Woodchuck," she said softly, "this may make your son the greatest of all horsemen. *Aiee*, to be suckled by elk-dogs!"

She chuckled softly and lay the baby down on a soft robe to sleep.

Even this breakthrough, however, failed to help Cartier's depression. He would sit quietly for long periods of time, staring at nothing, sometimes crying without a sound.

André became concerned for him. The man could not continue this way. They tried to engage him in conversation, but met only noncommittal grunts. Cartier spent much time behind the camp, near the burial scaffold with its blanket-wrapped burden.

André feared for Cartier's sanity. The band was preparing to move to the rendezvous with the other bands for the Big Council and Sun Dance. Could the sergeant be persuaded to leave this place of his bereavement?

As it happened, André was still trying to think how to approach the matter when Cartier himself solved the problem.

"Lieutenant," he said unexpectedly one monning, "I want to go home."

"Home?"

"Yes, sir. Mishi-ghan, or Quebec, or France. Just away from here."

"Of course, Sergeant. We start back in a short while."

"No, begging the Lieutenant's pardon, sir, I mean *now*. Tomorrow."

"But why?"

"I must leave this place, these people. I will stop to tell Cloud's parents of her death, and then go on."

"Well, I—this is quite sudden, Sergeant."

"Yes, sir. Would you have me take a report to Mishi-ghan? Then you could come later, after more exploration."

Well, why not? thought André. This would be a way to set at ease his concern for not having made any effort to return for over a year now. This would fulfill his military responsibility, yet let him pursue his exploration of the prairie for future settlement.

"Yes, Sergeant. It is good."

The odd phrasing of the People's language was creeping even into his French, he noted with amusement.

"I will prepare my journal," he continued. "You will deliver it to Captain Le Blanc as our report. I must finish a map and other directions. You wish to leave tomorrow?"

"Yes, sir, if I may."

"Good. I will work on the map."

Star had been listening quietly.

"I will prepare supplies for your journey, Woodchuck."

"Thank you, Star. I will not need much."

"You must eat, to travel. We have plenty. I will pack it."

"Good. Thank you."

"Now, Woodchuck, when you see Cloud's parents, tell them the child is well. We will see them soon at the Sun Dance. They can see him then. If they wish to raise him, he is their grandson. Or I will be proud to keep him. Tell them."

Tears came to Cartier's eyes.

"Whatever they wish. And I thank you and Sky-Eyes. Without you, he would have died already."

He turned away and went to choose his horse for the journey.

André worked a long time on his map, adding a note

here and there, making a correction. Then he reread the entire journal. How the world had changed since he wrote that first entry! Or how he had changed. He sat thinking for some time. There was something here that made him vaguely uncomfortable, but he could not define it. He gave a deep sigh. He only knew that his sworn duty demanded a formal and truthful report to his superior officer. He dipped his pen and began a final entry.

In summary, this land is ripe for colonization in the name of King Louis. There are many furs and game, streams full of fish and waterfowl, and immeasurable expanses of fertile land awaiting the plow.

It is in the best interests of the Crown that this land be claimed immediately. The map which accompanies this journal should point the way.

Respectfully submitted,
André Du Pres, Lt.,
His Majesty's Service

39
» » »

Sergeant Jean Cartier sat staring into his camp fire. The overwhelming loneliness that hovered in the darkness beyond its circle of light seemed heavy and oppressive.

Strange. There had been a time when the glorious open expanse of sky had been a thrilling thing. There had been excitement, anticipation in the grand experience. When he had shared the thrill of the future with Pink Cloud, everything had been pleasant and new.

The great dome of the sky, velvety blue-black from horizon to horizon, had been strewn with a million precious gems. The voices of the night were exciting too. The cry of the little yellow coyotes was echoed by the occasional deep hunting call of the larger gray wolf. *Le loup*, he and Du Pres had called them between themselves. *The* wolf. Their cry in the night was a startling thing, a shock that made the hair stand on the back of his neck. Yet somehow there was a comfort to the sound. It was a part of the mosaic of the prairie. It belonged there.

Just as, Cartier recalled, he had begun to belong. In the

past few months, aided by his wife and friends, he had
begun to feel himself a part of this unfamiliar world. He
wondered to what extent André Du Pres felt it. There
was good evidence that the prairie had changed the lieutenant too. He had adapted quickly to the skills and
customs of the natives.

The People had accepted the newcomers rapidly. It
was good to feel the friendly respect of the other hunters
for a job well done. There had been many congratula-
tions after the hunts. The People had rejoiced with the
young couple on the birth of their son. And mourned
with him, he recalled, over the loss of his wife.

"Woodchuck, my food tastes like ashes today," someone had said in sympathy.

It was a good description, he supposed. Weeks after his
loss, his food still tasted like ashes.

"You must eat, Woodchuck," Pale Star had told him in
parting. "It will keep your strength."

He saw little reason to keep his strength. What did it
matter now? The world which had just begun to open for
him and Cloud had turned bad. As bitter as ashes. What
was there now to keep one's strength for?

The great starry dome now seemed without meaning,
flat and useless, hovering over a great and useless land of
tragedy. The chuckle of the coyotes seemed to reflect a
ghoulish humor over his misfortune.

A great owl hooted his hollow call from the timber
along the river. *Kookooskoos*, Cloud had called the
creature.

"He speaks his name."

The call of *kookooskoos* had then been a matter of
pleasant, interesting conversation. It was now an empty,
almost supernatural sound, with tones only of hopelessness and foreboding.

Similarly, the night-bird who had called cheerfully *Pour
Pierre!* now asked the same question, but with a spirit of
hopelessness. Cartier shivered and tossed another stick
on his little fire.

It had been most difficult of all to tell Cloud's parents
of the tragedy. He had broken down in tears. The strength
and sympathy of Red Feather may have saved Cartier
from complete surrender to his grief, he realized.

He stared into his fire, watching the dancing pictures there. There are many stories in a fire, Star always said. She knew of such things. The world is full of stories, which sometimes inhabit the minds of people for a little while.

He shook his head. Everything had been so unreal since the death of his wife. He felt that he was living in a story. But which was real and which was the story? He seemed to be two people: Sergeant Jean Cartier, of His Majesty's army, on an expedition to the interior of the continent. He had spent a pleasant winter with a native woman to warm his bed, and was now going home.

No! screamed the other part of him. *It is not like that!* He was again Woodchuck, adopted man of the People, hunter, husband, father. Widower, he told himself sadly.

He wondered if he was going mad. He must have something to hang on to, something that would lend stability to this crazy changing world that seemed about to disintegrate in madness.

He sighed and shifted his position, turning a chilled portion of his shoulder to the fire. The oilskin packet in his shirt pressed against his belly, and he pulled it out to shift it to a more comfortable position. He sat looking at it dully.

Maybe this was his hold on reality. His military training rose into his consciousness. He must at all costs, even at risk of his own life, take back this report. It was the record of all that had befallen this ill-conceived expedition. It was his sworn duty to deliver it into the hands of his commanding officer.

Yes, if he concentrated hard on this as his primary mission, he could perhaps put behind him the rest of it. The delivery of the journal could close this chapter of his life and restore his grasp on sanity.

Strange, that one could hold his own life in the palm of one's hand. The slender, flat book held so much of importance. Cartier wondered what it might say.

Perhaps if he had not been at such an emotional crossroads in his own life, he would never have ventured to look. In his present confused state, however, Sergeant Jean Cartier of His Majesty's service did a most uncharacteristic thing. One he had never done before, and would not do again. There, at a camp fire a few days east of the River of Swans, he untied the thongs and began to read by the light of the fire.

The story unfolded before his eyes, the dangers and triumphs of each entry. Behind the formal, stilted language of the military report, he could see the thoughts and feelings of the man he had come to know so well.

The lieutenant must have experienced the same doubts and mixed feelings as he had. How difficult, Cartier reflected, for the hunter and warrior, Sky-Eyes, to write this report to his superior, urging settlement. The sergeant could see the doubt between the lines as he read. Duty demanded that the report be truthful and accurate, but the heart ached for the changes that it would bring to the prairie. The country of the People, the territory beyond the River of Swans would never be the same again.

He blinked back tears as he thought of the campground near the last resting place of his wife. Could he bear to think of loud and profane companies of soldiers and settlers camping there?

Her own people would not disturb her rest. Their spirit was one with hers, a part of her world. It was the outsiders who concerned him.

He rewrapped the packet and sat staring into the dying fire, holding it in his hand. The yellow-gray of the false dawn was showing in the east before he rose to replenish the coals. Dry sticks smoldered and caught fire, and the shadows retreated.

Cartier warmed himself, then sat cross-legged before the blaze. He took out the oilskin packet again, looking at it with new insight.

Carefully and deliberately he leaned forward and deposited the book in the center of the flames. He watched a few moments, while little tongues of orange licked hungrily at the oiled parchment. Then he rose to face the rising sun.

40

>> >> >>

The sentry at the gate of Fort Mishi-ghan's log stockade saw a movement in the distance and stiffened to a more attentive posture. He watched as the motion materialized into the figure of a man.

The traveler was clad in buckskins and appeared to have traveled far. There was something about the deliberate way he put one foot before the other that told of long distances. The newcomer disappeared for a moment in a bend of the trail, and reappeared again.

His buckskins were ragged, and differed from the usual local patterns, the sentry noted. The man carried a bow and a quiver of arrows. From the way he leaned slightly forward, he must be wearing a backpack.

The traveler's hair was braided in an unfamiliar style, too, catching the attention of the sentry. This man must be from one of the tribes to the west. New contacts were bringing people to trade now from new areas.

Then he noticed another thing. The man was bearded. Ah, one of the growing number of half-breeds, perhaps.

There was something vaguely familiar about the way

the traveler moved, the sturdy, deliberate stride. He continued purposefully up the rise toward the gate, and moved to enter. The sentry stepped to block his way.

"Halt!"

"Get out of the way, Chocteau!"

The man in buckskins shoved past him roughly to enter the fort. The sentry started to reach for a weapon, and then thought better of it. The glint in the man's eyes said that he would tolerate no interference. And how did the other know his name?

Chocteau hesitated a moment more. That gruff voice, the set of the shoulders—could it be?

"Mon dieu!" he cried. "Cartier!"

Sergeant Cartier paused and turned, somewhat apologetically, it seemed.

"We thought you were dead!" the sentry mumbled.

"I was, maybe. I am here now."

"The others?"

Cartier did not answer. He turned on his heel and strode on toward the Commandant's office.

He mounted the steps, not speaking to two soldiers by the door, and stepped inside. A startled clerk looked up from the desk, eyes and mouth wide in question.

"Sergeant Jean Cartier reporting," he said formally. "You would please inform the Commandant?"

The clerk nodded and scurried into the inner office. He returned immediately, followed by Captain Le Blanc. Cartier saluted smartly.

"Come in! Where are the others?"

"Dead, sir. All dead."

Cartier's lips snapped shut in a tight line.

"Dead, you say? *Mon dieu,* tell me! Here, come and sit. All of them? Brûle? Du Pres?"

Cartier took a chair and shifted his weight uneasily at the unfamiliar position. It was many moons since he had sat in a chair.

"Yes, sir. We capsized in a flooded river."

The captain opened a desk drawer and took forth a bottle and glasses.

"Cognac, Sergeant?"

"Thank you, sir."

Le Blanc poured the glasses half-full and extended one.

"Come, Sergeant. Tell me. You found the Water Passage?"

"Sir, the Big River we have heard of runs south, not west."

"Then—?"

"No, sir. There is no passage to the west. The river runs into the southern sea, the Gulf."

Le Blanc's face fell in disappointment. Cartier took a deep breath and plunged ahead.

"Captain, the land beyond is a desert, a place full of danger. The natives live in skin tents and wander from place to place looking for enough food to survive."

Disappointed as he appeared, the captain rallied to the occasion.

"It must have been perilous, Sergeant," he sympathized.

"Yes, sir. But we were proud to do our duty."

"Good man! Then you think there is no point in colonization?"

Cartier shook his head sadly.

"Begging the Captain's pardon, sir, but I would think not. There is nothing there that seems worth the risks."

"Yes. I see. Well, Sergeant, it is good that you have returned. Thank you for your report. Now, go and draw a uniform. I'm sure you will want to get out of those smelly buckskins."

"Yes, sir," said Cartier amiably.

He finished his cognac at a gulp and set the glass on the desk.

"Thank you, sir."

"Thank you, Sergeant."

Cartier saluted smartly and turned away. Outside, he paused for a deep breath. A tiny smile flickered for a moment at the corners of his mouth. In his eyes was a twinkle that had not appeared there since the Moon of Growing.

GENEALOGY

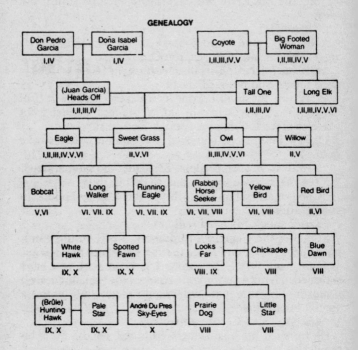

Dates for Volumes in the Spanish Bit Saga

I	TRAIL OF THE SPANISH BIT	—	1540-44
II	BUFFALO MEDICINE	—	1559-61
III	THE ELK-DOG HERITAGE	—	1544-45
IV	FOLLOW THE WIND	—	1547-48
V	MAN OF THE SHADOWS	—	1565-66
VI	DAUGHTER OF THE EAGLE	—	1583-84
VII	MOON OF THUNDER	—	1600-01
VIII	THE SACRED HILLS	—	1625-27
IX	PALE STAR	—	1630-31
X	RIVER OF SWANS	—	1636-38

Dates are only approximate, since the People have no written calendar.
Volume II, BUFFALO MEDICINE, is out of chronological order, and should appear between Volumes IV and V.
Characters in the Genealogy appear in the volumes indicated.

About the Author
» » »

DON COLDSMITH was born in Iola, Kansas, in 1926. He served as a World War II combat medic in the South Pacific and returned to his native state where he graduated from Baker University in 1949 and received his M.D. from the University of Kansas in 1958. He worked at several jobs before entering medical school: he was a YMCA group counselor, a gunsmith, a taxidermist, and, for a short time, a Congregational preacher. In addition to his private medical practice, Dr. Coldsmith is a staff physician at Emporia State University's Health Center, teaches in the English Department, and is active as a freelance writer, lecturer, and rancher. He and his wife of 26 years, Edna, have raised five daughters.

Dr. Coldsmith produced the first ten novels in "The Spanish Bit Saga" in a five-year period; he writes and revises the stories first in his head, then in longhand. From this manuscript he reads aloud to his wife, whom he calls his "chief editor." Finally the finished version is skillfully typed by his longtime office receptionist.

Of his decision to create, or re-create, the world of the Plains Indian in the 16th and 17th centuries, the author says: "There has been very little written about this time period. I wanted also to portray these Native Americans as human beings, rather than as stereotyped 'Indians.' That word does not appear anywhere in the series—for a reason. As I have researched the time and place, the indigenous cultures, it's been a truly inspiring experience for me."

A Proud People In a Harsh Land

THE SPANISH BIT SAGA

Set on the Great Plains of America in the early 16th century, Don Coldsmith's acclaimed series recreates a time, a place and a people that have been nearly lost to history. With the advent of the Spaniards, the horse culture came to the people of the Plains. In THE SPANISH BIT SAGA we see history in the making through the eyes of the proud Native Americans who lived it.

THE SPANISH BIT SAGA
Don Coldsmith

Bantam Books, Dept. LE10, 414 East Golf Road, Des Plaines, IL 60016

Please send me the books I have checked above. I am enclosing $_____
(Please add $2.00 to cover postage and handling). Send check or money order—no cash or C.O.D.s please.

Mr/Ms _____

Address _____

City/State _____ Zip _____

LE10—10/88

Please allow four to six weeks for delivery. This offer expires 4/89.
Prices and availability subject to change without notice.